SCANDAL

at the Willamina Quilt Show

by

Patsy Brookshire

Enjoy this romp with the quirky Willamina quilters.

Patsy Brookshire

Scandal at the Willamina Quilt Show

Copyright © 2013 by Patricia L. Brookshire

Published by
Ruby Rose Truckstop Enterprises
brookport@peak.org

Manufactured in the United States by Newport LAZERQUICK
in conjunction with Dancing Moon Press, Newport, Oregon

Front cover photos by Patsy Brookshire
Back cover photo by Linda Bancke
Edited by Judith B. Glad
Cover design by Jean Glassman

ISBN 13: 978-1-937493-48-6

Library of Congress Control Number: 2013914085

1. Romance
2. Murder
3. Mystery
4. Quilting
5. Oregon beach

FIRST EDITION:
AUGUST 2013

E-Published by Uncial Press,
an imprint of GCT, Inc.
Visit us at http://www.uncialpress.com

Dedicated to
John Lloyd Port,
With whom I share the keys, meals, and my life.

My thanks to these people who have helped me on this Scandalous journey:

Aunt Nellie Brookshire for your encouragement.

Deanna Rogers for giving me the title.

Fran Whited for helping me with your quilting expertise.

Deb Smith, for bringing The Quilter's Catalog to my notice and sharing it.

Sean Connor, without your help the fire couldn't have been put out.

JanniLou Creations Quilt Store in Philomath, and the wonderful women who accepted Jan and Lou's Quilt Challenge to make Sophie's quilt from my novel, *Threads*. Quilter's Cove in Newport, Judy Muller for helping with the fabric for the completion of the Scandal quilt.

With no-bounds gratitude I thank these women of my Oregon Coast Writers Focus Group who listened to every word: Marge Arvanitis, Kelli Brugh, Sunshine Keck, Mariah Matthews, Karleene Morrow. Your critiques continue to sharpen my writing and my mind.

To Writer's On The Edge of Newport, Oregon, for laughing in the right places.

To Rose Reed of LazerQuick in Newport, for your expertise and support.

To my excellent editor, Jude B. Glad. Thanks for your work, and to Uncial Press for bringing me into the e-publishing world.

To Greg and Bonnie Chaney for waiting twenty years for me to finish their wedding quilt.

My gratitude to my children Greg Chaney and Jennifer Chaney Connor is boundless. Thanks for believing in me and urging me on!

Chapter 1

Oregon State Fair, August 2008 Sunday Night

It was awful! Bugs moving everywhere, hissing. Frantically, with the other people in front of the cages, I was jumping this way and that, screaming and hopping about as the dang things flipped off the toes of my shoes. We never meant this to happen. But when our Exotic Bugs Exhibit of Madagascar Hissing Cockroaches started coming at us in a skittery flood, we couldn't stop and examine plans gone awry.

Sixteen-year-old Connor knew his roaches. His exhibit won First Place in its category.

I'm not a bug person, though I admire spider webs. It's kind of a crafty thing for a bug to do, weaving. But cockroaches don't do anything clever that I know of.

Those hissing bugs are humongous, some about the size of my cat's paw, the width of a silver dollar. They aren't like ladybugs, pretty and with poetry attached. I don't want any big ol' bug touching me. Eeuu. When one lands on my ankle and skittles up my pants leg, I jump with the crowd. I scream. I flick my leg. It falls out. And yes, I stomp it.

Right then a big broom would've been handy. Or a vacuum.

Connor, his father Dave, and I were only a few feet away

from the display, pleased with the number of people who crowded around the cages, until a man bumped into one of them, sending it smashing to the floor. I'd turned at the *CRASH* and saw the cage door fly open, throwing cockroaches onto the bare tops of nearby sandaled feet. A woman's scream pierced the room and the crowd recoiled. From the middle of the mass a man shouted, "Jumping Cockroaches!"

"Hissing Cockroaches, you fool!" shouted Connor, but the damage was done. The crowd, as they say, went wild. The cage emptied. Roaches bounced and crunched. People leaped. The air was blue with swearing as they scrambled, bruising each other's hips, toes.

Dave's voice boomed. "Calm down, everybody! The bugs won't hurt you!" But the crowd careened through the aisles, knocking exhibits awry as they passed.

"Dammit! Don't step on 'em!" Connor's shout overrode all, rising to a screech, "Don't squash them!" His frustrated, "Dammit all!" and then, "Shit!" rang through the disaster.

People slammed against each other, the mass of them folding and opening like an accordion as we swept down the long hall towards the closed doors at the far end.

Just inside these doors sat the U-shaped Oregon Authors table, which now served as the catchment area for our crazed, bug-fleeing crowd. Authors and buyers, mouths agape and eyes wide, stared. They recoiled *en masse*.

Leading us was a skinny and frantic woman wearing a fringed poncho. I saw her try to veer as she careened toward the center table that was laden with edible goodies. Instead, as if propelled by the wind of fear, she flew—until gravity prevailed.

She landed face down on the table. Arms outstretched she slid, sending home grown tomatoes, shelled filberts, Concord grapes, and slices of juicy, red watermelon in all directions.

Her slide ended in front of one of the authors who'd not run, but raised his camera.

I saw the flash but not the photographer. I'd been watching a flustered author wipe at her books with a soggy paper napkin, heard her moan to the man next to her, "So, who's going to fix this?"

He shook his head and popped a loose filbert into his mouth. "Not my problem."

What a mess!

I was happy. Most of the bugs were dead.

In the early afternoon I'd never dreamed that I'd be glad to see Connor's display thus, dead on the floor. It had started normally for a fair day, being day three of the eleven day-long Oregon State Fair, held in Salem, the state capitol. My young cousin had worked hard at putting together his display. What it is about these bugs that captures his interest I don't understand. But when they move slowly in their cages I am drawn to the color of their backs, a Halloweenie orange and black.

Earlier I'd heard a viewer remark, "I bet they'd shine up nice if hit with a bit of cleaner." I'd saved it to suggest to Connor that he should persuade his older sisters to do the job. I was sure they'd like to do that for their baby brother.

The blue ribbon reflected Connor's talent at showcasing the critters. His printed sign, *Have A Cockroach For a Pet!*, makes people grin and shake their heads.

I'd been thrilled when cousin Dave had asked me to help with this odd project. I had free time and enjoyed spending it with him, both of us hanging at the edge of our forties. My oldest cousin, Dave's father, Sam, was enlisted to help us with the daily sprucing of the cages, removing dead bugs and refreshing the exhibit with lively ones. In fact, Sam didn't help much, choosing instead to examine the baby chicken cage where he could flirt with their keeper, a pretty young woman.

He's a spry eight-seven. His eyes are not so bright with blue as when I'd met him nearly thirty years ago, and he takes his cane along for long walks, "In case I meet someone who should need it." His back is still straight, and he's a heck of a cook, especially with comfort foods, putting together a great homemade macaroni and cheese.

"I watch my energy. Need to save it for the ladies," he said, when Connor urged him to take a bug cage and clean it.

Yes. Well. Hmm.

When the bugs escaped and people went nuts, I was amazed how nimble Cousin Sam became. Flattening himself against the wall, he'd avoided the whole craziness.

To our rescue rode the roving man-and-woman-clean-up crew on their flashy bicycles, the man honking the bulb of his bike horn. Dressed as clowns, with white faces and painted smiles, they assessed the situation. His bike towed a maintenance cart stocked with brooms and dust pans.

Carnival music blared from the bike. The man turned off the music. Shaking her head, then her finger at us, the woman got off her bike to bow to applause. They were the perfect touch for our event. The man reached for a small push broom, looked again at the carnage, exchanged it for the largest one. The woman looked at the floor, turned down her mouth in an exaggerated frown at the bug litter, and took another large broom. They went to work.

When our blood pressures and breathing returned to normal, Dave, Connor and I grabbed tools and joined the clowns in mopping up. Connor kept making "Ooh, ooh," sounds.

Cousin Sam strode onto the scene to direct our brooms to little bodies that we'd missed. So helpful.

An hour later, the clowns stashed their tools back onto the cart, brushed their hands together, and jumped back on their bicycles. Honking their horns in farewell, they took away the bodies.

After a final check of the locks on the cages, we retired to the Exhibitors RV Area where Sam's Toyota Sunrader camper was parked for the duration of the fair. Gathered in what Connor calls, "Grandpa's trailer," we drank coffee and pop while eating Sam's stash of chips and salsa. We filled the place.

I finally looked at my white tennies, "Ugh, bug juice!" I wondered if bleach would take out the stains. I flicked the tiny remains of an orange and black body off my tan khakis.

"Sorry, Cousin Annie," Connor said.

I related the bug shining idea, which made Connor scowl until I suggested his sisters do the job.

"Teeny tiny brushes," he said, with wide-eyed teen innocence and a gamin smile. Affected, but effective. We all smiled with him, picturing his achievement-oriented sisters working on the bugs.

Sam balanced salsa on a good sized, lime, tortilla chip, and then tipped the whole thing into his mouth. "Hey, Connor! Ease up. T'wasn't serious after all, just an accident."

"Easy for you to say, old man." Dave was teasingly disrespectful of his dad, who responded by lifting an eyebrow at him.

Sam licked extra salsa from his upper lip. "I bet you can get some more of those roaches right here at the fair. At one of these food stands probably." He cackled. "Probably smear some of this salsa on the counter here, tonight, while we're sleeping and get yourself some more for the showing tomorrow."

"Oh, Grandpa, they're not those kinda roaches." He finished off his can of pop, and belched.

We all glared at him, which he ignored.

"For cripes sake, nobody got hurt. Except my Hisser guys. It's gonna take a couple days to get new ones. Tomorrow's Monday. We can get some from the critter store, here in town. Right, Dad?"

"Sure kid. Though I do like Gramp's idea of getting 'em for free."

"Whatever," mumbled Connor. Obviously the humor escaped him.

"Sleep for me. Connor, how about you and Dave taking the overhead? I'll bunk down here." I'd planned to go home to Gladstone but one more day here would be all right. I was too tired to drive and not on a time schedule.

We performed small-camper magic, folding the dining table out of the way, pulling out the seats to make a bed, couch cushions forming our mattress. Sam had his sleeping bag. From the tiny closet I pulled out stored sheets and blankets. Pillows for us both and we were okay.

A last trip to the RV Center's public bathhouse and I tucked myself into bed. Certainly not motel glitz, but all of us being snugged in here together comforted me. It had been over a year since I'd been to Cannon Beach where Dave, Teri and the kids lived with Sam in the old family cabin that they had remodeled into a comfortable home. Tonight was a treat to see and be with my relatives, young and old.

"Hey, Sam," I said into the dark camper, "Wanta come home with me for the week?" I live by the Clackamas River, in the house Roger and I built. But it is often too quiet. I like the noise of company.

My year-old black and white cat, Prince Charming, loves company too. He would be glad to see me home and to have somebody else to play with. Sam is a good animal man. His visiting me would give Dave's family some alone time, and respite for Sam too.

"Sounds good to me. Got an old friend in a care home up there, if you'd have time to take me for a visit. Sure would love to see her. It's one of those assisted living places. Never get me in one of 'em, but then I'm lucky to have family."

Sam had been a widower for many years, since his wife Sue had died in a hiking accident when she was in her sixties.

We decided that instead of my bringing Sam back to the Fair, he'd stay with me for a week or so. Dave and Connor would take his camper back to the house where it sat parked most of the time. He'd given up his driver's license but wasn't ready yet to let go of his vehicle, and it did come in handy for the family.

It took a while for us all to settle down. I eventually found a place on the firm bed that was comfortable enough to allow sleep. Despite Sam's whistling noises, as he slept, it was good to hear him.

Tomorrow we would wake up to a different reality.

Chapter 2

The Eyes Had It

We didn't see the photo until we heard the thud of the Monday morning paper on the camper's metal steps, followed by a knock and someone saying, "You might want to have a look at this." Connor was sitting in the front seat and he jumped out the door to retrieve the paper. He read the front page, scowling, and then handed it across the seat to his dad, who shared it around.

The bold headline shouted COCKROACHES ESCAPE AT STATE FAIR, and the photo, in full color, above the fold, made it impossible to not "have a look". The jumbled mess of flying books and food was all there. The most dramatic aspect was the glazed fear in the grey eyes of the woman sprawled on the table, her poncho askew, her forehead decorated with red watermelon smears, grapes tangled in her hair. The luck with the eyes made the photographer in me jealous.

I laughed at the grapes, but the guys scowled as they read the short article that suggested someone hadn't secured the cage. It stung.

Connor stood at the open door of the camper, flinging his arms about, punctuating the air with his energy. "Hey! Is that fair? The cage popped open when it hit the floor, that's simple enough. Why do people always have to make stuff up? They don't know why the door opened. Doesn't matter. None of us know! Stupid people!"

He stared again at the photo of the graped woman. "At least I'm not her! That's gotta hurt, her fifteen minutes of fame is a stupid photo of her being stupid." He walked around the trailer, three times, fast. When he finished he was breathing deep, slow and steady. He was a speed walker for his high school track team, and claimed it always helped him clear his mind.

"Hey! You know what?" he said as he came back in through the door. He took the paper away from Sam, who had turned to the crossword and was inking in the answers. Connor flipped back to the photo. "We made front page! Everybody will want to come see the hissers now!" With that he laughed and handed the paper back. "It's all gonna work out."

That is a great thing about the kid, he has a positive nature.

"Hey, Grandpa, do you have any frozen waffles?" With that we all got busy with coffee, cold cereal and toast, no waffles. After breakfast I went shopping for new clothes and shoes.

Dressed in my new duds, I returned to the exhibit to try to repair the damage with a photo of my own. I wanted to show the charm of the creatures, and to display the lock. I'd been sending my photos to venues around the state, and beyond, since high school. This was a perfect opportunity to use my contacts. I wanted today's photo to make the front page of the Cannon Beach paper. Though not the kind of publicity Cannon Beach High School was seeking, even bad publicity, as they say, is better than none at all. It's a small account for me, but, in family terms, it's big.

Connor was right. The crowd was here because of the story. I saw a man pull his rolled paper from his back pocket and quick-like place it on top of one of the cages so the headline was prominent. I left it there, thinking perhaps it would bring more attention. At least people were looking.

That's where I first heard of the Willamina Quilt Show, while staring at Connor's exhibit of the Madagascar Hissing Cockroaches, and wondering if my camera could capture how weird looking the creatures truly are. The only camera I'd brought with me was my small digital. I'd been thinking I'd only be taking family and State Fair snaps. But the little Canon would do well. It's just that when I am excited, I'm more comfortable with the familiar settings of my older film camera.

I was also intrigued by the photo byline, Len Bolder. Was it he, I wondered. The name was the same as a man I'd known long ago, but in all last night's excitement I'd not bumped into anyone familiar.

Nah, most unlikely.

I needed to focus. Ignoring the baby chicks in the Agricultural area, turning away from the glaring, glass eyes of the stuffed raccoons in the Wildlife Management area—gosh, the Fair was full of things to take my attention—I angled and zoomed at the cages, satisfied with their security. Using the dented cage as a frame I took a clear photo of the lock, and the bugs, within. Not so many, now.

Behind me I heard two women talking as they brushed past, caught in the crowd amassed in front of the exhibit. One was saying, in a determined, firm tone, "It's the best little quilt show in Oregon, maybe in the whole Northwest. Perhaps in the whole United States."

"Oh, Magda," a second unseen woman said, "Of course you'd say that, though I must agree. Our Willamina women do up a quilt show proud." The words became less distinct as they moved away. Probably going to the Jackman Long Hall, where quilts lined the wall, enchanting fairgoers with fabrics from flannel to silk, patterns from colorful geometric designs to abstracts. Each one different but each a demonstration of the love of quilts.

Several of my aunts quilted, but I didn't. I sew, but quilt? No. Too complicated for me.

Willamina? When I was an alcohol and drug counselor for the state, I'd had a client, a logger, from Willamina, a town somewhere just in off the coast. He'd snagged a Driving Under the Influence of Intoxicants—DUII. I do hope that poor drunk decided on a better life than the disaster he'd been working on at the time, starting with getting rid of that fridge in his garage stocked with quarts of cheap beer.

I'm taking a year off to assess what I want to do with myself when I grow up. The time off is the benefit of my late husband, Roger's, insurance policy. I shuddered and let it all roll away.

Magda's strong voice rose above the crowd's chatter. "This is a quilter's paradise. I always get lots of great ideas. I can't wait to see who wins Best of Show this year. Judy's art piece of Haystack Rock just stunned me and I know..."

Why she was stunned and what she knows was lost to me as their voices blended into the noise around the Unusual Bugs exhibit.

Tired of the crush and of holding myself in against the crowd, I flexed my thighs in the new blue jeans that fit so nice after all my workouts. The quick shopping this morning had landed me the Wranglers, red Crocs, and a red silk camp shirt. I wanted to look casual but sharp, just in case I saw Len, who I didn't know if I even wanted to see, but if I did, I wanted to look my best, casually.

"That danged Len," Aunt Sophie had called him. I hear her

voice of caution still. Many years since I last saw him.

Boy, it felt good to be smiling in spite of that photo in this morning's paper!

The photo. I couldn't let myself be distracted. *Focus.* A quick one of that little boy with the fuzzy yellow chick in his hands, his eyes alight. Who could resist? Back to the cages, and a highlight of the ribbon. The blue color is nice but, I doubted it would make front page.

I wanted a photo of the way the cockroaches' feelers branch about like teeny fingers, to show how "personable" they can be. Their value as pets.

The women's words returned to me: Haystack Rock? An art quilt of Haystack Rock? Did they mean the Haystack Rock of Cannon Beach, or Haystack rock at Pacific City? Both mammoth "stack" rocks were formed from boiling lava pushing up through a crack in the ocean floor to stack up, millions of years ago.

Ouch. My head hurts with the weight of the thought of it all...the agony of researching that paper for my college geology class. I'm seldom able to sit on the beach, peacefully sifting dry sand through my fingers, without thinking how deceptive all this serenity is. That my lovely Oregon has her sturdy haunches spread above the Ring of Fire; that underneath all the green trees and blue skies bubbles a volcanic hotbed.

From the corner of the wire cage I picked off a bit of black and red checked cloth. It looked to be a piece of Dave's shirt. Winning the blue ribbon was a Big Deal for the school, but the chaos these skittery little critters had caused yesterday for the Fair had become the real story. I hoped my photo, plus the ribbon, would counterbalance the drama these bugs had made in this morning's papers.

I checked the picture I'd just taken, a clear shot of the

padlock on the dented cage, and the surviving bugs, secured within. Satisfied, I worked my way out of the crowd. My stomach growled, talking to me.

Food. When a person is at the State Fair she must eat something bad-for-her, something one can only get at a fair. A deep-fried Twinkie? Maybe later, with the family. A corn dog was my first requirement. I headed for the nearest exit, hoping it would lead to the stall that sold the dogs.

Outside, the heat beaded up sweat on my hairline. The ground cover of dampened sawdust reflected the glare of the sun. Wincing, I put on my sunglasses. I walked past the olives on a stick, admired the various whirligigs turning every which way in the slight wind. All the while my ears were being pounded by the sound of screaming people on the Atomic Rocket.

Roger had loved the dang thing—he'd been gone over two years, to a disease that just wouldn't go away. I only had to dig my fingernails into my palm for a few seconds to short circuit the sudden, sharp gut pain. I moved it to the *later* part of my brain.

The enticing aroma of frying onions cut through the dust and heat. I turned to the nearest stall and saw a grill spread evenly with onions and sauerkraut for hot dogs. Beside it was a fryer for corn dogs. Fated.

My mind tickled me back to the Authors table. Len?

Maybe?

Perhaps I should let sleeping dogs lie. That would certainly be Aunt Sophie's advice. Best to check out the quilts back at the Jackman Long Building. Willamina Quilt Show? Maybe I'd find info there about it. *I must see that quilt of Haystack Rock. I wonder if it is anything like the one Aunt Sophie made?*

The line for corn dogs was long; I spent the time thinking about the problem facing me, at home, with another of Aunt Sophie's quilts.

And Len.

Chapter 3

Meeting Len

Aunt Sophie made many quilts but the one that the family treasured the most was the one depicting Haystack Rock at Cannon Beach. She had used the technique called appliqué, sewing cut-out pieces atop a base piece of cloth, to make a design. Upon a large, blue piece as background of the Pacific Ocean, she had created, with many other pieces, the rock and its surroundings.

Aunt Sophie's quilt, which now belongs to her son, my cousin Sam, has stood the test of time. It's still appealing to look at and cozy to wrap up in.

"Want your dog, Lady?"

I came out of my reverie to see the vendor handing me the corn dog on a paper tray. I fumbled for cash from my shoulder bag, took the dog. He pointed to the condiments on a small ledge by the window. I thought about mustard and decided against it—too dicey. Yellow against red silk would be awful.

I wandered among masses of people fanning themselves until I found the cool picnic grove of oaks and maples. From my bag I pulled a bottle of water I'd bought earlier and a small pack of chips.

While I ate my corndog and chips, I thought about the unfinished job waiting at home. I'd recently begun to go through the boxes into which I'd placed Roger's model ships. After he died, I couldn't stand looking at them. All those hours he'd spent on them, and I'd been jealous of the time. Now I just felt guilty. Why had I been so petty?

When I packed them I'd needed soft cushioning. In the chest Aunt Sophie had left to me when she passed, I'd found enough old blankets for the job. Ship number seven was the last one Roger had worked on and he hadn't finished it. All that was left in the bottom of the chest was a quilt. Aunt Sophie's last project, unfinished.

Great, an unfinished quilt, an unfinished ship. All the people I love leave things undone for me to take care of. I'd wrapped myself in self-pity while folding her quilt, pins and all, around Roger's last ship.

Now I wanted the space and didn't need to hang onto the ships anymore. A new maritime museum in Newport had expressed interest in ship models for display, so it would be the perfect place for them. They were all true miniatures of real ships that had sailed the seas. The completed models were all in a box, waiting to be transported to Newport. The partial quilt remained in the chest, wrapped around the unfinished ship.

What was I going to do with the ship? Or the quilt?

I threw away the lunch remains and walked to the Jackman Long Building, passing the Oregon Authors Table. Giving it a quick glance, I didn't see anyone I knew and went on to the Quilt Display.

The display dominated the whole room, with quilts hanging from all four walls, as well as being on frames on the floor in the main fabric crafts area. On the walls the quilts

16

were high enough so they couldn't be touched, but low enough to read the tag attached to each one. In bold black letters was the name of the quilt and quilt maker, and from which Oregon county it came. Blue or white or red ribbons were attached to winners of the County Fairs around the state, and most of them had garnered more awards in the statewide judging.

They were beautiful, all sizes, shapes and designs.

My neck was getting a crick in it as I stared at a particularly intriguing one, labeled *Tumbling Blocks*. It was the illusion of three-dimensional blocks made by the piecing of dark triangles against lighter colored ones, that amazed me. *Now just how was that done?*

Impressed, I had pulled out my camera to take a photo, when I felt the weight of a hand upon my shoulder.

"Are you sure you want to do that?"

I turned to shake off the hand and stared into Len Bolder's face. Older than the face in my memory, but the same dark eyes with extra long lashes. Face tan and weathered.

Len. I swallowed and gathered my cool. And took the photo. "Len. It *is* you."

His eyes swept me in a frank once-over, his smile lifted his sharp cheeks and deepened the dimple beside his mouth.

I restrained the impulse to put my hand to his lips and then to the dimple. I'd forgotten just how cute he really was, or is. I felt my face freeze into a wide-open stare, let out the deep breath I'd been holding, and grabbed his hand.

His fingers curled over mine, lingering upon and then leaving my ring. "Hey!" He pulled me to him in a hug that I returned.

Inside me there was a loosening, but with the tiniest pulling of hairs, like when you pull off the rubber band you put on your wrist to store it for a while.

"How in the heck are you! I've been over here at the Authors Table—Oh, have you seen my book?—and I thought I saw someone who looked like you pass by our table and go into the quilts. I talked the guy next to me into watching my place while I came looking."

His top lip covered his bottom one for just a second, in a manner that I fondly remembered meant he was thinking about what he was going to say next. "Are you here alone? 'Cause I could be gone long enough for us to have a cup of coffee and catch up...if you could?" He was obviously wondering about my marital state.

I told myself I shouldn't be judgmental. I'd had a flash of regret of having the ring on when I realized he would have the wrong idea. I had left it on at first for reasons of love, and then sentimentality. I was still wearing it now because it kept men at bay.

"Uh, sure. There's a place outside."

"Oh, I know where it is. I have a Thermos. I'll grab it and a couple of cups."

I was full of questions, and I felt the trepidation I always felt when I had to tell someone about being a widow and how I'd become one. I didn't like talking about it.

He led me back to the Authors table, grabbed the jug and two cups from the center area that had been neatened up from last night's debacle. He also grabbed a copy of his book. I caught a quick flash of the title, *Hunting For The Perfect Photo*, with a photo of him sitting in a duck blind wearing camouflage, camera raised.

I wondered if we'd have enough time to talk about both his book and my widowhood. We had bugs and the photo to talk about too. He wasn't wearing a ring. Some men don't wear one because they work with machinery.

He introduced me to the man next to his spot, Joe, who said, "Didn't I see you last night in the bug mess?"

"You were here for that?" Len said.

I told Joe that yes, I'd been there last night. We chatted a moment until Len lightly took my arm.

"I'll be back. I just need to catch up with this lady. Been a long time." I pulled my arm from his hand and moved from leading to watching him walk in front of me. His butt cheeks shifted nicely against the thin cloth of his brown cotton trousers.

The flame began then to rise within me, a heat I'd not felt for some long time. I remembered my fingers on the sweet place under his lip, touching and tracing and kissing it. With that small heat began the seeds of the scandal that was in time to overtake me and the Willamina Quilt Show women.

Aunt Sophie was surely looking at me from the ether with that knowing shake of her head. I ignored the hint of my own caution, and plunged ahead.

Chapter 4

Len and The Willamina Women

"Married?" I asked him as he poured coffee into our cups.

"I'm not cut out for marriage. Things have been better since Lin and I straightened that out. But..." He looked at me with a wry grin. "...we see each other a lot. We have a business and we work together. You're wearing a ring, so where's the lucky guy?" He looked around as if expecting to see him stroll up.

"Not here." I fumbled at my wedding ring. "Not anywhere nearby." Plunging into the present, I twisted the ring, and pulled it off. "You remember Roger Straw?"

His nostrils flared. "How could I forget?"

"I don't think he ever forgot you, either." I said, with a short laugh. "We were married for twenty-three years, and he died a little over two years ago." I shrugged as he watched me playing with my ring, turning it and putting it on my middle finger, pulling it off, admiring the diamonds in the simple round of the wedding circle as they flashed. "Haven't felt like taking it off." I returned it to my finger. "It's silly and sentimental to still wear it."

"Sorry to hear it. Nice to know you two lasted. Kids?" He

took a big gulp of his coffee.

"No. Just never happened. Neither of us really cared, though. Not enough," I amended, "to do anything serious about it." I felt no need to recount the yearning years. They had passed with time. "I have nieces and nephews. That's enough for me. You?"

"A son and a daughter. The perfect family, though somehow we could never hit the mark—Linda and I, I mean. The kids are great. It was a relief for both of us when we went our separate ways." He shrugged his shoulders at the modern term for divorce.

"The kids were young. Harry and Sandra stayed with Linda most of the time but we did a lot of stuff together, camping, weekends, and, you know, stuff. Our relationship is mostly through the business."

"Business?"

"You'll never believe it. I write and take photos of events. Like the Fair here."

He smiled ruefully as I shook my head. He'd hated that when we were together I was aiming to be a professional photographer. It took time away from him and I'd smelled of developer chemicals. He'd said that when we got married I'd have to give it up because he "...wasn't going to have a wife who smelled like a chemist."

"I know. But it just happened."

"Does she develop the prints?" I couldn't help it.

"Ah, she did." He rushed past that, "We do most of it digital now, on computer. You know. It's different."

Most? I wondered just how gone she was.

Aloud I said, "Yes, I do know. I'm in the business, too. I'm still taking pictures and shopping them out. Makes us in competition, huh? Funny."

"Yeah, funny." He raised his eyebrows at me, shook his head. "We also buy and sell arts and crafts, sort of an import-export business, except we don't go beyond the U.S. borders. She's off in Alaska right now, visiting her sister who's married to one of the native guys there, head chief of the village, or something.

"Say! They're both quilters, Linda and her sister, Pam. They got me into it, which is why I'm wondering just what you were doing looking at the quilts? You one of us?"

"'Us? You quilt?"

"Sure. Doesn't everybody?"

I pulled the remaining water and chips from my bag. This quilting thing was like a curse that was following me around. "My Aunt Sophie quilted."

"I remember that. A house full of them if I remember right."

"I sew."

"Therefore, you are."

"Don't be silly. I don't quilt." The noise of the Fair seemed exceptionally loud, even here in the little picnic grove.

"Speaking of photos—" I'd suddenly remembered just why I'd looked him up, "You took that one of the woman on the table last night. It's great but I wasn't happy with the attention to our little accident."

He'd just started to peel a banana he'd pulled from his own small bag, and his grin transformed his face into happiness. "Yes. Wow, wasn't that a hoo-rah! That woman made a mess of our table and didn't even buy a book." He finished peeling the banana, offered me half, which I took. "But what do you mean, 'our' little accident. How were you mixed up in all that?"

I told him the whole bug story. "So you see, 'our' is practically my whole family. Connor just about had a kid coronary when he saw that photo and the headline this morning. As did we all."

"Well, don't that beat it! My little snapshot is what brought us together." Somehow he is always the focus, the main deal.

I'd wondered if the world still revolved around him. Apparently it does.

"I'm glad I caught your eye, however it happened. Did I tell you that you are looking fine? You were always sweet, but you've grown up real nice. That red shirt does fit you, and you always were a good blue jeans gal. I've often wondered... Hey!" He shifted gears. "Dinner, on me, tonight. Heck, bring everybody. Corn dogs, my treat."

I love his laugh. It comes from his whole body, beginning with deep rumbles from his belly, rolling up his esophagus, pouring out his throat. It bounced around the grove. People around us looked our way and smiled. He has shorter laughs but this was the best, his completely happy laugh.

"And then we can talk about quilting!"

At least a new line. Gotta give the guy credit.

"I'd love to, but tonight I'm going home, taking Sam with me."

His expression darkened. "Sam?"

"My cousin, Aunt Sophie's boy." Did he remember the family relationships?

"Oh, Sam." He smiled, nodding in remembrance. "Sampson. He's an old guy, right? You met him when she told you about him? Her baby." He gave his shoulders a quick shrug, dismissing Sam.

"Say, where do you live, anyway?"

The tables in the grove were all filled, and I could see a family looking for a table. "How about going back in and looking at the quilts? I was looking for one in particular, from Willamina. We can talk where I live, and all that, inside where it's cooler."

"Good. Because I do have a need to know. Willamina? I think they're doing the afternoon demonstration in the County Quilt Booth. Wanta go talk to them?"

"Yes!" *Lord, this man is a treasure trove of info.* "Where's the booth?"

He led me back inside, past the cake decorating and the vegetable displays, past the lace making, to the County Quilting Booth. It was near the Authors Booth and had a rotating display of quilt making put on by different state counties. He told me these next couple of hours belonged to Yamhill County, represented today by Willamina. I could hear it before I saw it. Women's voices, giggles and loud laughter.

One woman's voice rose above the rest. "Come to the Willamina Quilt Show. Best little quilt show in Oregon." I recognized her voice from yesterday. Magda. She was standing inside an enclosed square bordered by piles of quilts, handing out an information sheet. Inside the square, several women were sitting around a quilt stretched taut on a frame, their hands busy pulling thread through the cloth with tiny needles. It looked for all the world like a 1900's quilting bee.

I took one, glanced at the map on it, and then at her.

Her body was sturdy and her face, with half glasses resting on her nose, was happy. I immediately liked her.

"When is it and where? I mean, of course it's in Willamina, but when?"

"Oh, honey, it's in November," she said. "See the date here?

24

If you want to enter our Challenge we have a section open to people not from Willamina. You have lots of time."

"How do you know I'm not from Willamina?"

"Sweetheart, I know every quilter in Willamina. There's not that many of us."

"How about me?" Len said.

"You? Well, I'm sure I don't know what about you." She moved so she was standing opposite him, with the piled-up quilts between them. "You want to enter our Challenge?" She was staring at him over her eyeglasses, challenging him. "You can, you know. We welcome men. Some of our best quilters are men, but right now we don't have any. I'm surprised at the wonderful work you guys can do. After all, men aren't much into detail and quilting is all detail and patience, and—"

"You bet I quilt! Doesn't everybody?"

"Maybe not 'everybody'. Some of us might have other things to do," I said, feeling defensive, excluded. I stood straighter, wiped the churlishness from my tone. "I think it's great that you quilt, Len. Just not my thing."

A tall thin woman came to stand by Magda. "This guy giving you trouble?" Her hair was a perfect coif, a sausage roll like I'd not seen outside of photos of women from the Forties, a smooth folding of hair that framed an angular face. These women appeared to be of my generation, which made me wonder just when and how they'd started quilting.

The desire to quilt had certainly passed me by. It was something old people did. Wasn't it? I remembered why I'd wanted to talk to these women.

"...trying to get into our show."

"Well, we just might let him," the thin one said, "but he's got to show us what he's got, first." She tilted her head flirtatiously.

I didn't care much for this flirting. "I have a question. Magda?"

"Yes, I'm Magda Buler. This is Lena Veil."

"I hear that you have a quilt of Haystack Rock."

They looked at each other.

What was that about. Maybe they don't understand what I'm referring to? I clarified my question. "At Cannon Beach?"

At that another woman came from the center of the square. "What do you know about a Cannon Beach quilt?" She pursed her mouth at Magda and Lena, and they both stepped back.

"Hey, Sunshine, we didn't say anything," Magda said.

I said, "I'm sorry if it's a secret. Yesterday while working on the Bug Exhibit, I heard a couple women mention a quilt about Cannon Beach and I have reason to wonder what it looks like. I thought it sounded like your voices."

They both laughed and relaxed a bit.

"Okay." Sunshine said to me, "We'd appreciate it if you didn't spread it around, but it's not a big secret. We just don't like the competition to know too much before the show." With that she went back to the side of the quilt frame.

Secrets? I wondered what the big deal was. A quilt's a quilt, isn't it?

"How does the competition work?" Len said. "Do you have to be a member of your Quilt Guild to enter? Or," he added, his manner unusually humble, "a woman?"

Why, I wondered, did he want to know?

While Lena dealt with his question, Magda took me aside. "You say you don't quilt, but I think you have a question. What is it?"

"I had an aunt who lived at Cannon Beach and made a quilt featuring Haystack Rock. 'Applique,' she called it."

"When was that?"

"Right after the first World War. I was wondering what your quilt looks like."

"It's not my quilt. I'll tell you this much. One of the other gals has something. If you want to see it you'll have to come to our show."

"Look, we don't have time today, but I'd like to know more about this quilt."

We were getting off my question about the mystery quilt, but I didn't notice, not then.

"Is it still around? Could I see it?" said Magda.

"Sure. I'd like to show it to you." I'd have to get it from Sam. That wouldn't be a problem. I knew he liked to show it off.

"And I think there is maybe more you have to ask?"

I nodded. Could she read my mind?

She reached into her back pants pocket and pulled out a card. "Here. All my info is here. I teach quilting, and I also authenticate quilts."

At my questioning look she pushed her card into my hand. It had a quilt design on it. "Just call. Part of authenticating is registering with the state. A quilt like that needs to be recorded."

I tucked her card into the side pocket of my purse, an innocent enough act.

As we were leaving I noticed that Len was holding a piece of paper. "What's that?"

"While you were gabbing I entered a quilt in their show."

"What quilt?"

"Tumbling Blocks. You were looking at it when I found you."

"You made that?"

"Hey! Your family isn't the only one that quilts, you know. And yes, I am proud of it."

I said, "You should be. Boy, you are a surprise! Now, maybe, I'll have to go to the dang thing."

Hard to imagine Len as a quilter. The little I knew of quilting led me to think it required, above all, patience. Even Magda had mentioned it. He'd always been short on that.

But then, people do change. I sighed to myself with relief, thinking of our distant past. I was going to count on it.

Chapter 5

Sampson Speaks

I didn't expect to live this long, not this long without Sue. She was the light of my life and sometimes I think this dark is going to last forever. Gotta say, though, I have found ways to get through, to be happy in this time without her. I know, things change.

Like me. I've had to adapt. People in the old days had to learn new stuff, trains, phones, all that. I'm making my way. When the kids presented me with the idea of using a computer, I balked, but they brought the dang thing right in the house with us and so, I got curious.

Learned it, although one day when it came up with some message about me committing some Fatal Error, I got on the horn and called Dave up at work. Luckily he was in the office and not out driving the truck or I'd' a said a couple things to Teri that a woman doesn't need to hear.

"Kid! If you don't get home pretty damn quick here and help me with this thing I'm gonna take a hammer to it. Then I'm goin' on to Walker's computer next door, smash it, and then wherever. This crap has gotta stop!" I meant it, too. I was so mad!

Dave told me to take a walk on the beach until they could get home. So they got me on board with it all and now I help other people. Like my friend Kit in that care center where I'm going next week. I'm over eighty but I'm not done yet.

Something Annie doesn't know about yet. I met Magda at the Fair. In truth, I met Magda some years ago when she was at Sophie's Cabins, probably about 1980. About the time I met Annie.

I liked her then, but I was married and I didn't fool around. Besides, she was at least twenty years younger than me. She was married too.

Maybe she flirted with me then because of my blue eyes. Like Paul Newman, I'd like to think I'm more than a pair of eyes. She did flirt with me though, not seriously, but enough so that when she showed up at the Bug Exhibit looking for Annie we sort of recognized each other.

"You look familiar," she said.

"Oh, you say that to all the bug guards," I teased, and then reminded her of her beach visit about thirty years ago.

"I can't believe it! You remember me after all these years? I don't even look the same! I was skinny." Her voice boomed, making the bugs jump.

She does look different, has put on a few pounds. Looking good. I shook my head at her, and said, "Still look the same to me. Better. I like a woman with a bit of meat on her bones. Bones are for a dog, the meat is for a man."

That stopped her in her tracks, for a minute, and then she laughed.

That was what had attracted me way back when, the boom of her laugh. The bugs didn't like it, I could see them getting nervous. I took her elbow and moved her away from the cages, over to a bench by the open doors.

She sat down. I sat right beside her so I could hear her over the noise of the carnie rides outside the door.

She didn't move away. "I'm sorry," she said. "Your name? It's been a long time." I started to tell her, but she put her hand on mine where it was resting on my leg.

"No, let me guess. It's unusual, but not."

I kept my hand right where it was, didn't want to waste the moment. It's been a while since I've felt the warmth of a flirty hand on mine. I watched Magda's face twist comically.

"Joe? No, common, but not." Her brows folded, before she smiled widely. "Sam! For Sampson! The guy with the hair! The strong guy."

I put my other hand over hers, squeezing gently. "Well, I'm older but I'm still strong. Strong enough for normal purposes."

"Oh, Sam." She'd pulled her hand from mine and was now pushing my chest with it, soft like. She even colored a bit. "Uh, how's Sue? Isn't that your wife's name, Sue?"

"Yes. It was. I mean, she's been gone for a long time now. Died some years ago."

"Oh! I'm sorry, Sammy. I liked her. She was a jolly soul. Made our time at the cabins really nice."

That reminded me that she'd not been alone on that vacation, but not with a husband, but her husband's sister. Joan, that was her name.

"So, how is Joan?"

Her eyebrows rose. "You remember her name?"

"I didn't forget yours, Magda. So how's her brother? The guy who picked you girls up?"

She laughed again. "You sly dog. You are still so cute. My

husband Tommy?" She pushed her hair off her forehead and ran her fingers over the top of her head. "Wow, warm isn't it!" She straightened, leaning her head away from me. "Aw, he's okay. He's gone a lot. I quilt a lot. We get along okay."

"Well, I'm sorry to hear it. Where does he go?" I couldn't help grinning.

"He's a fishing nut. All the time. We have a boat. I sometimes think the boat has him. He doesn't even like to eat fish. He just fishes. Whatever's running, he's out there chasing it."

"You get lonely?"

"Just cut right to the chase, eh?"

"Sounds like you're alone, but not? Does he have a gun? Do you play around?"

Magda stood and held out her hand to me as if to give the old guy a helping hand up, if he needed it.

I didn't. My turn to laugh. "Just thinking of your options. Quilting's great. Mom Sophie made her living quilting, but I always thought she needed a boyfriend. You know, to take jars off lids, and stuff."

"If I remember right that was the name on the cabins, but seems to me that your mother's name was Amy?"

Before I could answer, she continued. "Tommy is a good guy. He's just not there. Never has been. About a year ago he took off on that boat with a friend of his. They went to Mexico to fish and are still there. He's not much on phoning. Heard from him on New Year's Eve. He was drunk. Lord! No, I'm not lonely. I have my quilt friends. I'm busy. And for the most part, happy."

This was a funny conversation to be having by the open door of the Jackman Long Building. I brought it back to why she'd come over to the Bug Exhibit in the first place. "Weren't you looking for my cousin, Annie?"

"Annie's your cousin? What a coincidence. Maybe that's why she seemed familiar to me. You do share a slight family resemblance." She stared at my face. "In the cheekbones. Kinda Nordic, or is it way back Indian?"

Lord, she was starting to go woman on me, wanting to examine the details. "I don't know. We can talk about it later, if you want. Right now I need to get back to my Bug Protecting Detail. Some of us have to work, you know." I broke us a path through the mess of people heading out the door. "About Annie. You want me to give her a message?"

"No, I'll call her. I have her number. We have a quilt to talk about."

"I'll be staying with her next week, so perhaps we'll meet again." I wasn't going to let her slip away from me twice. The other time had not been a possibility but, now, here, I sensed something. "Maybe you could give me your number? Do you ever come to the coast, anymore?"

"I live in Willamina. Quite a ways from Cannon Beach, but not so far, if a person wants to swing by."

I didn't like to have to say this. *Dammit, I hate getting old!* "Look, the fact is, I don't drive anymore." We moved through a clot of people. I was glad for the diversion.

"Okay." She smiled, and when we got to the Bugs, she gave me a hug. "I think we can figure out a way to meet up again. I'll be calling Annie. You tell her I was here. This is for you." She gave me her card. "You will hear from me."

She walked away and I stood there, by the bugs.

Hmmm. Did what just happened, really happen? Is she still flirting with me, after all these years? I walked over to a couple looking at the Exhibit. "These are Hissing Madagascar Cockroaches, you know," I told them, feeling like I needed to talk to someone, tell them something. I'd liked feeling important even if it was only for a few minutes.

When they walked away, looking at me like I was a little strange, I decided it was time for me to go to my camper and start packing, check my wardrobe. I've got a nice blue shirt that I know the ladies like.

Wonder if I brought it along.

Chapter 6

Me and The Trunk

On Monday I played the afternoon away with Dave, his wife, Teri, and their grandchildren. The fair was more fun with the kids, Amber and Krysta. By the end of the day we were all hot, and sticky with their cotton candy, and yes, we'd shared one deep-fried Twinkie. The girls judged it, "All right." No one needed another. It was a fun afternoon. Sam, who had spent much of that time at the camper, packing, and I left in the early evening for my home on the Clackamas River. As much as I love traveling, I treasure even more coming home to the forest and the river.

The river is a dramatic backdrop to the backyard of my home. It's why Roger and I bought this property and put our dream house here. It's a wild river, full of life, despite a dam upriver. Clear water scrambles over large and small rocks, foaming white as it drops into small pools. At the river's edge the water swirls around low-hanging branches, twisting and tearing off leaves and pine needles as it ambles here, speeds there, moving freely on. All of it pleasant to look at and listen to.

From my back porch or from windows that I open on warm nights, I hear the river wending its way to the Willamette.

35

The sounds are calming and yet stimulating. Now, as we near Autumn, the slowed splash from the lowered water level helps to cool my fevered mind. This business of meeting up with Len had me in a spin. And that unfinished quilt of Aunt Sophie's nagged at me in a way I hadn't expected. Something had to be done with it, but what? I didn't know which was troubling me more.

After a good night's sleep, the week with Sam had an interesting twist, causing me to wonder if my aunt was haunting me. She was with me more than I'd felt in many years, because of Sam? He was a greater spur with the quilt than I'd expected, starting with asking about Roger's ship models.

Tuesday morning I told him I'd come to terms with letting go of Roger's ship models, but that I had a problem with one of them not being done. "I hate to just throw it away." I said.

"Can I have a look at it?" He said. "I haven't done one of those in years, could be fun to finish it for you. Or him."

We spent the morning in Roger's room. Sam patted the trunk. "Mom's old trunk. I'm glad you have it." I lifted the lid and he stared at the maroon and green quilt wrapped around the unfinished ship. He took a sharp breath.

"I remember this quilt. Mom started to make this for our wedding, when Sue and I got married. But she never finished it. Don't know why. She made a traditional *Wedding Ring* instead."

Before I could stop him Sam bent down and wrapped his hands around the clumsy bundle. I needn't have worried. His touch was as gentle as if he was lifting a newborn baby. Underneath was the original box that the model had come in. I took it out and closed the trunk so Sam could set the blanket-wrapped ship on the lid. He stepped back to let me unwrap it.

"She made our *Wedding Ring* with Sue's color scheme of

orange and gray. I think she said this one just didn't go. Sue used to kid me that as long as my mother's *Wedding Ring* covered us I'd never stray."

He pulled over a straight back chair and straddled it. "She never had a wedding ring, you know. Mom didn't." I thought of his tangled childhood, living with his father, David, David's wife, Amy, and David's other love, Sophie, Sam's mother. He was only two when Sophie left him to be raised by Amy and his father. Sam took a deep breath, went back to his tale of fidelity, taking pride, I think, that he'd been a faithful husband.

"Never even wanted to, though some fine women came to the cabins. Temptations. I know that a couple, or more, were looking for a fling and..." He trailed off, his arms wrapped around the back of the chair, his eyes on the quilt, watching me separating the unfinished quilt top from the ship, making one pile of ship pieces, another of connected and loose squares of cloth.

I'd thought this was a completed top, just not yet finished into a quilt. "Ouch," I yelped and pulled a pin away from my finger, sucking at the welling of blood.

"Gotcha, did she?" said Sam. "Gone, but not forgotten."

As I continued, carefully, taking the squares apart I found that few of them were sewn together, leaving more loose ones than I'd thought. To make room, I moved the ship pieces into the model box, set it on the floor. I spread the quilt pieces on the top.

The deep maroon pieces were velvet, lovely to pet. My fingers massaged the nap.

Sam picked up another piece of velvet, ran his hand back and forth, watching the color change from dark to light as he flipped the nap, smiling. Sewn to some of the velvets were squares of light brown corduroy, the same size, printed with small flowers. I made a pile of loose, leftover squares, wondering if there were enough to finish the top.

In the middle of the bundle was a piece of notebook size paper. On it Aunt Sophie had drawn the plan for the quilt. "Well! This will help."

"Sure would be nice to see it together," said Sam. He'd picked up the ship and I thought he meant that. But he put out his free hand and, again, stroked the velvet.

I just stared. How was I to make any order of this mess?

"I'll help you with quilting, if you want," I remembered Magda saying at the fair. I'd said "No" at the time, being sure I didn't want anything to do with this. Now, I was wondering, just what would it look like if it was all put together?

I said nothing more to Sam about the quilt, but put him onto setting out the ship pieces on Roger's work table. "Look, here in this drawer are his glue and modeling things." He was easily diverted and spent much of the day working on the ship. I was happy that he was doing it, but watching him handling the pieces was unsettling. I left him to it. It was the next week before I discovered that Sam had taken it home with him. It was a relief.

I must be out of my mind. "One of the Willamina quilters said she'd help me put it together, if I want. In fact, she gave me her number."

Sam looked at me, as if it all seemed simple to him. "So, call her."

"I've got a lot of things to do."

"And all the time in the world." He rolled his eyes. "I'd sure like to see it done," implying that it was the least I could do for my old cousin.

"Now," he said. "Call her now."

On her answering machine I heard the strong voice I'd first heard behind me in the crush at the Bug Exhibit. Sam leaned to the phone to listen. "Hello, Magda here. Today I'm at the Fair so if you leave your name and number, I'll call you back. Meanwhile, keep stitching." Her laugh ended the message.

At the beep I did as instructed, and said, "I met you at the fair. You wanted to know about my aunt's Cannon Beach quilt. So call me." Sam glowered at me until I added, "And maybe I want you to help me with one of her other quilts."

I hung up and said, "Maybe. But don't count on it."

"What a good voice." Sam wasn't referring to mine. There was a light in his eyes that disturbed me.

"Sam, what's going on?"

"Nothing. I forgot to tell you that Magda stopped by our bugs booth when you weren't there. We discovered that we knew each other from way back, when Sue and I were doing Sophie's Cabins. So, we're old friends. That's all."

I considered. "Sam, I think Magda is married." I didn't mention the age difference, and I didn't know her marital state but I'd seen her plain wedding band. I noticed things like that.

"So?" He stepped back. "Her voice reminds me of Sue. Strong like. Not many women speak like that. And what if she is married, what's that got to do with me?" He ducked as I passed the phone close by his ear to smack the receiver into the cradle.

"Sorry," I fibbed. "Just don't be trouble."

"Don't you worry, sweetheart." He laughed. "Frankly, I think we could both use a little spice in our lives." Whatever did he mean by that?

I spent the rest of the day catching up on laundry, playing with Prince Charming, leaving Sam to himself. After dinner we watched TV for a while, the cat curled up beside him, then I said, earlier than usual, "Time for bed. We gotta get up early if I'm to get you to your lady friend by noon."

"Yes, indeedy. And maybe we'll get a phone call."

While getting ready for bed, I pondered his use of, "We." Was that the royal 'we', or, did Sam have plans that might embarrass me?

Chapter 7

To Willamina, A Drop Back in Time

Wednesday morning I woke to the smell of coffee and toast. Above it all floated the aroma of bacon frying. Bed to bathroom to kitchen. An easy track. My kitchen is U-shaped. At the open end, below the multi-paned window, is a table. Sam was setting plates as I came in. "What a treat!" I said.

He went back to the kitchen for the coffeepot and cups. "We'll see if it's fit to eat," he said, as he came back with a cup in one hand and coffee pot in the other. "Coffee, Madam?"

At my grateful assent he poured a cup.

"Cream, madam?"

"Sam, you are just a little too silly. No." I waved off the offer. "We don't have any anyway."

"I couldn't find eggs either," he said as he set our plates before us. He had found the almost empty jar of orange marmalade that I hid from myself, to be used in emergency.

"It appears that you are my emergency." I folded a piece of toast over a couple of the slices of bacon and bit into the sandwich, alternating with gulps of the coffee.

"Not sure what you mean by that," he said, while putting marmalade on his toast, "but we've sure enough got urgency, this morning."

I waited. Everything seemed to be right in my world. He kept smearing marmalade onto every bit of toast surface.

I caved first. "What urgency? The toilet, or the shower? Oh, please, I just can't stand to hear that anything is leaking. Or worse." It had been a summer of plumbing problems, but I'd had everything fixed.

He wasn't talking about plumbing.

"Willamina. We're going to Willamina. Today is perfect. Look out the window." He pointed to the gorgeous scene just beyond the window. A light mist was rising from the river as the cool water from the mountain met the warm morning air. I slid the bottom part of the window open to take in the misty breath of the river. It was invigorating, carrying a hint of autumn.

Sam stood up, empty plate and drained cup in his hands. "Whaddaya say?"

I closed the window. He was right, it was perfect weather for a day trip. But I thought he had other plans. "You want to take a country drive today? You've got your friend Kit to visit, remember?"

"I've taken care of that, talked to her this morning. We'll visit Kit tomorrow, or Friday, if you've got the time."

"Oh, heck! I've got more than enough time. Why are you so hot to go to Willamina? "

"Magda's expecting us."

"Expecting us?"

"She said today about noon would be good."

He took my cup and plate, put them in the dishwasher. "So, hop to it. You get your shower and dressing out of the way."

He closed up the dishwasher. "Why waste time?"

I couldn't believe he'd already talked to her. But he had and he'd scheduled my day. Maybe bringing him home with me wasn't a good idea. Action, he's always been about action and was dragging me into his plan.

Funny thing, I was ready to go. The events of the last few days had wakened me. I thought, if going to see a quilter was exciting, I could increase my thrill—I have Len's number, too.

It didn't take me long to get ready, but Sam was ahead of me. When I opened the car door he was already in the passenger's seat. He was wearing a blue checked shirt that I'd not seen before, paired with his khaki pants. His hair was combed, not something we always saw. His silver hair was his true crowning glory, full and abundant and usually flyaway. Today he was looking spiffy.

"Hey," I said, "You're looking good."

"Oh, you say that to all your old cousins. People always tell me that I'm looking good, nobody ever says I'm good looking." He settled into his seat, pulled his seat belt snug.

My jeans and thin rust-colored sweater and new tennies looked dowdy beside his glamour. I'd pulled my hair back into a short braid at my neck.

My reluctance to leave my wooded home was strong as usual, I like to nest once I'm there, but Sam's nagging got us on our way. By eleven-thirty, temps in the Willamette Valley were climbing. I had the air-conditioner on until we were past the humps of the Coast Range, approaching the Willamina turnoff.

"Do ya mind if I turn this off?" Sam's fingers were hovering over the AC switch.

"Heck, no. Open your window."

He did. "Oh, gosh. This feels better. Okay, slow down,

you're gonna make a left right up here."

I'd seen the sign. I'd forgot how irritating a back seat driver can be, no less so just because he's sitting right beside you.

As I drove into Willamina I felt like I had dropped back in time. Just beyond the turn were several huge piles of logs, bark still attached, and beyond that about twenty empty log trucks side by side, their log beds doubled back in park position, like grasshopper legs.

Sam had been quiet since he'd seen the frown on my face when he'd directed me where to turn. "That's where Dave bought their first truck, got a good deal on it, too." Seeing the trucks reminded me of my ride on a log truck with my Uncle Ray. "We were coming down from the far hills below Mt. Hood where the snows drain into the Clackamas, to a mill in Estacada.

"Whew-ee! That was quite the ride. I was nine or ten. I'd been out in the woods with my best friend, Dorothy, where her dad and his crew were building roads in the backcountry. He was a Cat driver.

"But that ramming ride down the mountain, twisting around the trees alongside that gravel road, with Uncle Ray blowing his horn before corners, but not slowing down any—I was holding onto my teeth the whole way, let me tell you!"

As I was speaking, we passed a lumber mill, surrounded by stacks of logs, with red numbers painted on their ends. Beyond them were tall, neat piles of cut lumber, ready for shipping. And hovering over it all was an orange mountain of sawdust.

"Now that's some sawdust!" said Sam. "Did I ever tell you how Sue grew up with a sawdust furnace in her basement. She'd fill the hopper before going to school in the morning and all day feel the sawdust itching down her neck."

Willamina's a true lumber town. The restaurants all have a lumberjack theme to them. No tree-hugging signs here to suggest a green park from which to take a life-restoring walk in the forest. I laughed to myself.

"Where do I turn, now?"

"You're gonna like this. Take a left here, we're going into the country."

"We're already in the country."

"Straight ahead. At this next fork, now, turn right. Uphill here. Past these black and white cows, just like she said. Keep going. Then these horses. Whoa! Slow down here."

I wasn't going fast.

"Yup, here's Quilter's Lane. 'Spect she named it herself, you think?"

Speaking of gravel roads, some crazy man on a Cat had carved this one out of the forest. Sliding off the road and getting stuck out here with an old man was not in my plan. Who would push? I was getting heartburn. "Sam, in the glove box. Get me a Tums."

He found them, fished out a couple. "This do ya?" I ignored him beyond a 'thanks', chomped it down. A little ways on I was reassured to feel the gravel become solid macadam. We came around a little bend in the road and there it was, a Hansel and Gretel house. Or the Witch's—but made of wood. Gingerbread would be goo in Oregon rain. Cute as could be. Flowerboxes below the two front windows, overflowing with nasturtiums. Yellow mums filled the flowerbeds at the skirt of the house, with blue and yellow violas at their base.

I parked in front of the garage. Out the front door came Magda, smiling broadly, barefooted and glorious in a yellow blouse that reached to her hips. Under that she wore close-fitting tight black stretch pants with thin black lace at the hem.

"Well, howdy," she hollered, "I wondered if you'd find the place. Hi, Sam. Miss Annie, isn't it? Glad you brought her."

"Oh, heck, Maggie, your directions did the trick."

"Maggie"?

His step was firm as he took her outstretched hand, gripping it longer than I thought need be.

She let go of his hand and reached out to give me a gentle hug.

"Come on in! We'll have some tea and talk. It's been a long time."

With that we walked into a quilter's paradise.

Chapter 8

Magda's Thoughts

I love my studio. It's a place of refuge where any interruptions are planned by me. Once in a while something happens outside, like the bear at the apple tree last night, but that I'm tickled by. I expect some wild animal behavior up here. It's one of the reasons I picked this place.

This morning I saw mess around the tree, mushed apple remains and the ground torn up where he sharpened his claws on the trunk. I expected to see bear butt marks on the seat of the picnic bench where he'd sat while he finished off an apple. The image of the bear leaning back against the table with his legs crossed, flipping the core into the trees, made me grin.

Tommy says I'm fanciful.

My husband, Tommy, is a charmer, and so busy. He built the table to give himself a place to work on his gear when he wanted to be near me, but after a while he couldn't stand the quilting anymore. I couldn't get anything done with him in the house and he was just about nuts with my fabric everywhere and the occasional stray needle in a chair.

He hated that. Well, who can blame him? So we came up with two solutions, my sewing studio here in the woods, and his boat.

He's older than I, enough that he's completely retired and can fish as much as he wants. Okay with me.

He's always checked in with me every month, but I haven't heard from him for more than two. My calls to his cell went to voice mail for a while, but now it doesn't connect at all. So he's either gone to Mexico and got himself a Mamacita or gone to Davy Jones. I say "was" because I think the boat has gone down. The Coast Guard hasn't reported any sunken boats, or sightings of anything like oil slicks or debris.

Been near a year since I've seen him. Doesn't make that much difference, sorry to say, in my life. He's either here or not. I've learned to take care of myself. But yes, I'm lonely. Companionship would be nice.

Chapter 9

The Studio, and Sausage Rolls Hair

Magda said, "Before we sit, I have something I want to show you." We followed her to a large room, a sewing studio. On the far side was a tall window, illuminating the opposite wall. Sitting by that wall was a quilt on a simple frame. An old quilt was laid over the top of it, to protect it I supposed, from dust and the wide beam of light. The light brightened the opposite and side walls that were lined with shelves filled with bolts of cloth, full of color and bold print. Tiny flowered print. Stripes of all colors and widths. Solid shades of the rainbow and the artist's palate.

"I've never seen so much material in somebody's house before!"

Magda gave me a funny look. "It's fabric."

"What?"

"The material. It's 'fabric.'"

I wanted to say, 'Well, la de da. Forgive me for being so old fashioned,' but I realized from her smiling expression that she was explaining, not mocking.

Sam walked over to the frame. "Do you mind if I look?" He began to lift the old quilt off the one being worked on.

Into the room strode a woman with a cup in her right hand. It was Sausage Rolls Hair, from the Fair. She shoved his hand away from the frame. "Whoa! Wait a minute there. Unhand my quilt."

I couldn't tell if she was mad or joking.

"Lena! It's okay. He's not hurting anything." Magda said.

Sam bristled. "I wasn't gonna hurt the damn thing. Just wanted a look. Who are you? Is this yours?"

Magda said, "Let him see it. He's not going to hurt Judy's quilt." To Sam and me she said, "This is Lena. We share the shop, we work here, together. It belongs to me." She hesitated. "To Tommy and me."

"If you say so." Lena set the cup down on a small table nearby and began peeling the old quilt off the frame.

"I'm confused. Magda, you said it's Judy's quilt, but you..." I nodded to Lena. "...say it's yours?"

"Lena is quilting Judy's beach quilt here for the show. Lena, I met Annie and Sam at the Fair."

Lena held the old quilt rolled in her arms. "You," she said to me, "I remember from the Fair. You were awfully interested in a Cannon Beach quilt. Somebody tell you about it?"

I laughed. "No. Remember, I heard Magda talking about it with one of your other quilters? That's why I came over to talk to you."

Magda took the old quilt from Lena and motioned her into a chair, "Sam, here, is from Cannon Beach. That's why Annie wanted to know about it."

"There's more to it than that," I said, while Sam stood staring at the quilt on the frame.

"It's The Rock!" He reached out to touch it.

Lena reached to push his hand away. "Don't you know better than to touch a quilt?"

He jerked his hand away, saying, "Don't touch a quilt? How you gonna put it on your bed? What if the cat jumps on the bed, or, heaven forbid, your dog?" He was winding up. Lena and he were like electric hot wires, flashing off each other. I thought of the effect she'd had on Len.

Len. I wanted to call him. But I didn't have a reason why. Not one that sounded plausible. Not one that wouldn't sound like I was fishing for more than just a chat.

"I don't have a dog. My cat is a Hairless Sphinx. I don't have hair in my house, and I certainly don't have good quilts lying about on the bed. If you were to come to my house, which isn't likely, you'd see my Specials on the walls. Or rolled and wrapped in old sheets for storage, as should be."

"A Hairless *what*? Maybe, lady, you need a dog. Your attitude could be useful. You could take that stick outa your butt and throw it."

Magda stepped between them. "My Lord, it's a quilt, not a gauntlet.

"Sam, take a look at this. Lena is the best hand quilter I know. Check out these stitches." She motioned to me. "Annie, come here."

Only part of the quilt face showed. Most of the top and the last bit of bottom were rolled under so that Lena was working on two and a half feet of quilt. The top of Haystack Rock was rolled under but the base with the tide halfway around it was still recognizable as one my favorite places in the world to walk and breathe and listen to the birds squawk at each other fighting over bits of clam or crab.

"Sam, you could stand to learn a thing or two and become

humble, at least about what you don't know. Quilt humble."

We both looked to where she was pointing to the stitching around the base of the Rock. Tiny stitches.

"See, count them." She pulled a small ruler from the deep pocket at the hem of her shirt and laid it on the material—uh, fabric. "Twelve stitches to the inch. Perfectly outlining the base of the rock where it rises from the sand, suggesting that the water is moving."

We looked. The stitches were so small as to be nearly invisible, pulling just enough at the cloth to bring suggestion of movement to the piece.

Sam reached to trace the stitching, but Magda's hand stopped his, gently, as Lena said, "Don't touch!" He pulled it back but without the anger that her remark alone might have spurred.

"It's nice. You do good work. I gotta admit it." Sam said.

All I could think was, how does she do this?

At Sam's compliment Lena's feathers laid right back down again. Her moods appeared to change quickly.

"Oh, it's nothing. You could do it, if you wanted."

"And I don't!" he said, laughing.

Magda said, "Would you like some apple pie? I made one up this morning from that tree out there. That dang bear didn't get them all. He sure tore up the ground, though, where the kids next door moved the table. They got some apples for their mom and left a tubful for me, so I made a pie."

"Sounds good to me," said Sam, "Miss Prickly here could use some sweetening."

Before Lena could answer, Magda took his hand and he followed her out of the room. "Coming?" she said over her shoulder at us.

52

"I want to look at this. Be right there. Lena, how do you do this?"

"Carefully, one stitch at a time. But it's not so hard, I've been doing this since I was a child. My grandma lived with us and she taught me. She was the best quilter in the state!"

"Looks to me like you must be that, now."

"I do my best." she said.

"Could you teach me?" What was I saying?

"Not me. But that's why you're here to see Magda, isn't it? She's a natural at it. If you got something to learn about quilting, Magda's your teacher."

Is that why I'm here? Or am I parting romantic waters for Sam?

Chapter 10

A Surprise For Me

We sat around the kitchen. The apple pie was possibly the best I've ever eaten.

Magda said, "When I was growing up I made pies for my mom's restaurant downtown. It seemed to be the only talent I had. These are fresh apples and a tad overripe. I let myself go on the sugar with a good dollop of nutmeg and cinnamon mixed with butter. The sugar, spices and juice mix to make a lovely sludge. Of course I can't tell you the secret of the crust." She rolled her eyes to the garbage where she'd tossed the pre-made pie crust wrapper, and let out that laugh again that gurgled up from her tummy.

Sam joined her. I was laughing with them when Lena came in.

"Oh, whew!" Magda slowed her laughter.

Sam said, "Oh, boy! Nothing I like better'n a woman who knows how to cook old fashioned. Here, sourpuss." He pushed out the chair beside him, "This pie will sweeten you up."

Lena glared at him but set herself down. She cut a slice of pie and slid it onto the dessert plate Magda handed her.

"Coffee, Lena? Fresh from the Thermos. Made it this

morning." Lena started to rise.

Sam put his hand on her shoulder and got up instead. "I can do that. I'd like some too. Cups?"

Magda pointed to the open cupboard and he took down two cups. "Annie?"

I wanted tea so Magda put on the teakettle.

"Did you say a bear'd been at the apples this morning?" Sam said.

"Boy, howdy, yes! I think I just missed him, musta run off when I slammed the back door. The pile he left for me was still steaming."

"Oh, Mag, we're eating here!" said Lena, but the pie was doing its work. The corners of her mouth were twitching upwards. She took another bite of pie, "Pretty good pie even though it's almost too sweet for me."

I swear she simpered at Sam. What was with this woman? Five minutes ago she was glaring at him.

The whistle of the tea kettle interrupted this sudden coziness. Magda poured hot water into the teapot, let it steep for a few minutes, and filled my cup.

Sam had watched Magda's movements in the tea process. "Could we go out and look at your orchard? I'd like to see where the bear was, and to have a gander at your yard."

I thought that he'd also like to be alone with Magda.

"Just a minute. I'm almost done here." Lena shifted in her chair as if she was ready to get up.

"You just take a rest here, we'll be right back." When she threw a questioning look at him, he winked. "Oh, Sweet Pea, I'm sure you don't want to see bear shit."

"Oh. Yeah." She settled back in her chair. "Not finished

with my coffee yet, anyways. You two be careful where you step. I noticed earlier that the boys used the table to pick the apples. That will need to be moved back to where it was."

They didn't hear the last part because they were going out the back door. Magda was laughing at Sam, who'd said something about the bear fertilizing the lawn.

While Sam and Magda walked around the back yard, we could hear their muted voices through the screen of the open kitchen window, see Sam leaning against the table while he watched Magda pick up apples and put them in the tub the boys had used.

Lena and I cleared the pie things, and she took me into the master bedroom that I'd seen on the way to the ocean quilt. I thought I knew what the large contraption in the middle of the room was. "Is this another quilting frame?"

"Yes, a longarm, for machine quilting."

"Machine quilting? I've heard of it, but this is huge. Is this yours or Magda's?"

She had just answered, "Magda's," when Sam and Magda came in. She asked him, "Did you put the picnic table back where it belonged?"

Magda answered her, "Oh, we forgot. It's okay the way it is. Oh, good. Annie, you've seen what we'll probably end up doing your quilt on."

Lena said to herself, "No matter. I'll do it myself. Later."

"Huh?" was all I could say.

"Sam told me about you finding a quilt of his mother's that you need to finish."

I continued to stare at her, and then snapped my mouth shut, opening it only to say, "Sam!"

"He's out in the car, bringing it in so we can get started on the plan, see what we will need to do to finish it."

I didn't know we had the quilt with us. That Sam can be a sneaky sort.

"News to me. Why am I always the last to know? And I don't think this is going to happen. I don't quilt." I heard the car door slam and lickity split Sam was back in the room with us, holding a large paper tote with "Cannon Beach Groceries" printed on it. The very one he'd been using for his dirty clothes.

"Here we are." He was smiling ear to ear, pleased with himself. "A surprise for you, Annie, my girl. Magda's gonna help us."

"Us?"

"Yah, you'll finish the quilt."

"And you're going to do what?"

"Watch. Encourage. Be happy when I see Mom's quilt done."

Magda said, "You could enter it in our quilt show." Those two were off and running.

"Have you two been drinking out there under the apple tree? I thought there was a process involved to get hard cider!"

They ignored me. "Here, Sammy..."

"Sammy?"

"Put it here on this table, let's have a look."

He upended the tote onto the table, spilling out the pieces of velvet and corduroy. Magda began squaring them up, sorting the material into like piles. "Nice. Oh this will be interesting to make up." She looked at me, surely noting my twisted mouth. "You are going to have such fun. And with these heavy fabrics you will be better off machine quilting it."

"Me? Machine quilt it?"

57

She was ignoring me. "Oh, I like these flowered prints. Corduroy. Haven't seen such for years. You know, fabric runs in fads, like clothing styles."

"Before anybody quilts this you must teach me." I spread my hands over the spilled cloth, suddenly feeling proprietary over the pieces.

"Don't worry, honey, I'll do it with you. Sammy here can help us."

I remembered my one sewing class in high school Home Ec and my frustration as the teacher had, over and over, said, "Annie, you must rip that out."

I'd made an apron and a blouse and a simple dress. All had been so painful with the amount of ripping out and re-sewing that I'd not sewn much since. At Christmas I get inspired to make simple gifts, pillowcases and placemats and such, but I'd found someone who I could pay to do our mending and Roger had been okay with it.

I quailed at being dragged into this world of quilting. But, my ego wouldn't let me hand this over, either. I equivocated. "No, wait! It's all too tricky."

Magda put her hand on my shoulder. "Not 'tricky', Annie. A little hard to begin with, but once you get on to it you'll see it's wonderfully easy and so relaxing. You'll never know all the problems I've solved just by sewing them away."

Chapter 11

Sewing Away the Winter Blues, With Len

Magda said to us both, "I trust you brought your mat, grid rulers, and rotary cutter with you?" I stared at her, then at Sam, whose mouth dropped open.

"Uh, what?" he said.

"Your tools! Quilting tools. It's no matter, I have plenty here, just that some people like to use their own supplies. I bet you forgot your sewing machine, too."

I turned on him, accusingly.

"I figured you'd have needle and thread and scissors. What else could she need? I never even heard of those other things, whatchamacallits, and, rotary cutters? None of this is for me, it's for you, Annie." Sam turned to me, as if eager to put this all back on my plate, even though he'd started the ball rolling by bringing Sophie's unfinished quilt.

"Well, no matter. Let's see what we have here and what we need to do." Magda's matter of fact manner relaxed that ache between my shoulders.

"If you'll help me I'd like to get it finished." I said. In response she handed me a round, flattish bowl with a magnetic center. In it were long pins with flat yellow heads. Easy to grab and to pin with.

All my quilt pieces were there and already cut.

Magda smiled at me. "I knew you had the makings of a quilter!" Her hands were slapping the pieces around in different configurations, when her fingers seized on the old piece of brown notebook paper printed with gridded squares, the paper that I'd found when I had first looked at it—Sophie's diagram of the quilt. I'd forgotten it. Written across the top in Aunt Sophie's careful penmanship was *Sam's wedding quilt*. I'd missed that in my initial, quick inventory.

In pencil she had labeled the simple drawing of the triangles and squares of her design with the kinds of fabrics to be used: "velvet, corduroy, cotton", and named the colors: "purple, flowers", and so on.

Magda, examined it. "This is certainly going to help," which is what I'd said when I first found it. Using Aunt Sophie's pattern, we laid out the pieces on the large table.

"What size do you want this to be?" She smoothed out the pieces. "Perhaps you want a sashing between these blocks?"

At this Sam started inching away. "Uh, I'll just be outside. Want me to pick up some more apples, Maggie? Maybe move the table?"

She stopped smoothing. "Hold her Newt! Young man, this is your project as well. You're gonna help here."

"Oh, Magda," I said with a laugh, "I don't think Sam knows much about this business."

"It's high time he started taking responsibility for finishing what he starts."

I wondered if she was just talking about quilts, but let it slide when he reeled back into the room as if she had a string on him.

"What do you want me to do? I can wield scissors with the best of them!"

"Twin, queen, king?" She nudged me. "Bed size, Annie. What size do you want this quilt to be?" She walked around the table. "Sophie was just working it out herself. Discovered she didn't have enough fabric. You want a wedding quilt to be large enough to fit on a double bed, or a queen."

She pulled a small chart from a drawer "Okay. Your first decision. What size?" I took the chart from her, looking at numbers that meant nothing to me. I knew my bed at home was a queen, and picked the numbers under that heading. "Eighty-four inches by ninety-two inches."

Magda was still talking to herself, but listening to me. "So she switched to another style that she must of had enough fabric for."

I went to hand the chart back to her.

"Keep it. You're going to need it at the fabric store." She went back to shifting the pieces around. "This is going to be complicated because I don't have any of this velvet or corduroy fabric. She bought them to match but didn't get enough. The whole thing got unwieldy."

She led us back to the first room, gestured at the shelves of fabric lining the walls. "We'll see if I have what you need. Let's start here. Are we going to sash it, or add the width and length to the outer edges?"

She explained sashing. "Each square is framed by one connecting fabric. Brings it all together."

I found that I did have an opinion. "Oh, no! I don't want it broken up. I want Sophie's original design to stay as it is."

"You're going to need to add fabric. Accept it." She led us

to a colorful pile of bolts of cloth on a shelf. Here, help me pull these down. Put 'em on the table." We worked free several bolts of different shades of red and a multicolored cotton with tiny splashes matching the deep red in Sophie's velveteen.

"The easiest way to lengthen this to a Queen is to put a large border around it, extending it at the top and bottom."

"For interest and eye appeal, it's best to bring your contrast and color all the way to the edge. It needs brightening up for a modern look. I like a splash of good color. Don't you, Sammy?"

He looked at her, goggle-eyed, shrugged his shoulders.

She pulled out a pen, started calculating how much more fabric we would need. Math. My stomach lurched. My brain was beginning to spin.

My cell phone rang. "I'll just take this outside," I said, but they weren't paying attention. They were busy playing with fabric options, with numbers, with each other. I was glad for the call.

"Hey, Sweets."

Len's old nickname for me. At his voice I felt a tiny glow start.

"I have news for you."

Chapter 12

Balancing Act

"Where are you right now?"

"In Willamina, working on Aunt Sophie's quilt."

"Willamina? Wait a minute, isn't that where those Quilt Guild women are from? Are you hooked up with them? Honey, I can teach you whatever you need to know."

"About quilting?"

"Sweets, I can show you a lots of things I've learned since I saw you last." A low and teasing tone.

Hmmm. Perhaps I should take him up on this.

"Well, even though I already know everything there is to know, perhaps even I could learn something. About quilting." We set a time for the next day. I would take Sam to his date with his friend at the care center, leave him there and meet Len at an old house he was remodeling.

"It's kinda rough, but I think you'll like the place. And I'll show you my etchings... I mean quilt setup. I have some tricks that I'd love to teach you."

I could feel prickles of sweat pop out along my spine. He'd always had that effect on me. I would plan to pick Sam up in a couple of hours. That would be plenty of time to feel Len out about quilting, and who he'd become. Maybe learn something?

And I would have a reason to leave before I compromised myself. Maybe.

When I went back inside, Magda got right to the point. "Now Annie, I don't have a lot of time, but you, and Sammy of course—I couldn't get used to "Sammy"—are always welcome here, and we must get cracking on Sophie's wedding quilt so you can enter it in the Quilt Show."

"What quilt show?"

She laughed. "Our quilt show, of course."

"Oh, I don't think so, Magda. I don't know a lot about quilting but I know to be in a show a quilt has to be just about perfect. And I'm certainly not going to hand quilt it." The Quilt Show was in mid-November, part of a town-involved project, The *Coastal Hills Art Walk*, to kick off the Christmas season. It sounded like fun, before I'd been told that I might be part of it.

I was both attracted and repelled by the idea. I certainly wanted to get the quilt done for Aunt Sophie. Doing it was beginning to be attractive, a challenge that, maybe, I could do. If it didn't turn out well, I could always refuse to let it in the show.

"Doesn't need to be hand quilted. You'll enter it as machine stitched. I'm on the committee, it will get in. I'll make sure you do a good job."

On Labor Day we'd come for breakfast, on my way to taking "Sammy" back to Cannon Beach. We'd set a time for my first lesson, then.

Sam was delighted. His few days with Cousin Annie was working out well for him.

Chapter 13

Magda's Thoughts

I must admit, Sampson is appealing. Is it his hair?

I joke. I am a married woman. I need to control myself here. And for gosh sakes, he is an old guy. Oh, but he does not look or act old to me.

As for Annie, she needs my help for sure, and there are few things I like to do more than teach someone how to quilt. It is a skill that has strengthened me when nothing else could. Gives me a challenge at the same time it soothes me.

I've needed it as Tommy has been a trial, this marriage was most likely a mistake but I could not, would not be dissuaded when my mother warned me about his wandering ways and his wandering eyes. He told me that only I could make him whole, settle him down. I did want to believe him.

I also chose not to pay attention to his drinking. My best girlfriend, Loyola, warned me. "Maggie, he is not the same person when he's had a few. You know he flirts with all your girlfriends. I fear the fights he gets into at the bar. For you."

"He won't be doing that when we are married," I told her. "He has promised me." I was only eighteen and "ready for love," as they say. He was twenty-four and, he said, "Ready to settle down. I've had my share of women and, yes, wine, but you and I together, we'll make a team that will keep me on a steady course."

Loyola had just shook her head. "But what if he gets mad at *you*? His temper is awfully quick."

I brushed that off with not even a thought. I wouldn't let it happen.

Our marriage worked for the first couple of years, with some, yes, crunchy times. I've since learned with alcoholism, that was the best of times. Ever since it's been a struggle. The day came when Tommy did hit me.

We were arguing, standing toe to toe. Both of us were shouting, I don't even remember what about. He told me to shut up and I shouted back, "*You* shut up."

He raised his right boot and stomped down on my left foot. Hard. I thought he'd broken something, it hurt so bad. I screamed, and it scared him, so he backed off.

I hobbled over to the phone and shocked us both by calling the police. One of the two officers who came to the house that night was an old school friend of mine, Wish Kelly. That made Tommy madder. He knew I'd dated Wish in high school. He tried to tell the cops that I'd hit him first. I denied it and Wish believed me.

He said, "Tom, if I ever even hear of you hurting her again, you will go to jail. Magda, I'm putting this on record of you filing a complaint. If this or anything like it ever happens again and I'm not around, you make sure the arresting officer knows about this report. And Tom, listen up scumbag. You better hope I never come here again because I can't promise you'll make it all the way to jail."

After Wish left, all Tommy said was, "I told you to shut up."

He never touched me again, but that was really the end of our marriage. I didn't trust him. He tried to talk me into moving away, saying us living in this place was like living in a fishbowl. My friends and family were always interfering and as long as we lived here we'd never have a good marriage because of it. I'd think about moving, and then I'd step wrong and my foot would hurt, and I'd remember.

We stayed together but with trust gone, it got so I didn't like him anymore. I was glad we didn't have kids. We had a lot of years of living together but he went his way and me, mine. Way back then everybody figured it was the woman's fault if her husband hit her. She wasn't doing something right, and, besides, where was she going to go? It was ugly. It's better now, but still hard.

For us, Wish stopped the violence right there. I guess being threatened by a man with a gun was more powerful than anything else I could have done. And Tommy knew I'd call. He blustered a bunch, but he always stopped when he saw the look in my eye.

Once he got the boat and started fishing, that helped. He's gone for months, and I'm glad of it. Maybe he's dead. Wouldn't be a terrible thing. Sad, yes, but he's not been happy with life for many years.

I probably should divorce him, but I just hate to give up. I miss the young Tommy, do have hope he'll show up again. I miss his wry sense of humor, and our adventures together. I look at our surfboards on the wall, and remember excellent times. Perhaps? If he quit drinking? I'm optimistic. I did say, "For bettor, or for worse." But now, it's easier with him gone. Plus, our financial lives are intertwined. We own the house and everything together. Selling the house and giving him half would be good for him, but not for me. I could move into the studio, but I like having my home life and my quilting separate. I have a peaceful life.

For now I've got this job of teaching Annie to quilt, and that will be a challenge. Such resistance. And Sammy. Oh he's a handful! Yes, indeed, he is.

The quilt show is in November. We gotta get cracking. Time to put the needle to the cloth.

Chapter 14

The Heat of The Valley

Thursday

Sam's first question the next morning at breakfast was, "What time are we going to Valley Home? I need to give Kit a call."

"As I recollect, I'm taking you there for lunch, so yes, you'd better call her. I'll drive over to meet Len and pick you back up about one-thirty."

"So he really is back in the picture, huh? Your picture. Not mine. Frankly, you know Mom didn't much care for him. Was so happy when you settled down with Roger." He cleaned up the last of his oatmeal.

After a morning raking leaves, giving the yard a quick spruce, we headed to Valley Home in Portland. Len's house was an easy fifteen minutes from there. After I dropped Sam off I worked my way through lunch hour traffic.

All this hunting to find places, I need to buy a GPS.

I was wearing a crisp yellow linen camp shirt over wide-legged tan shorts. Blue earrings and a silver heart necklace. Sandals with yellow socks. My hair loose. I checked the visor mirror. Yes, my pale mauve lipstick was holding up well. I ran my tongue over my lips, thinking of the way Len's hips had moved in his shorts. Lord, he was still a good looking man!

His place was down a gravel road off Marine Drive. The house was about a hundred years old, from the look of it.

We had had a complicated history of physical intimacy. I'd wanted it but was afraid, too. I'd always been reluctant, up to that certain point where I joined him in his passion. Then, after, guilt, and the fear of pregnancy.

He'd been irritated, assured me that the condoms he used would work. It certainly wasn't satisfactory lovemaking, but I was young then. He'd had some expertise, but wasn't much beyond me. It had all been about him, but I hadn't known the difference, then.

I wondered if he had improved. I knew I had. All those years of marriage to a man who loved me with passion and care, the difference being in the *care*. Now I expected more of Len, and of myself. I looked forward to our encounter.

Before I could knock, he pulled the door open. He was dressed in the same shorts he'd been wearing at the Fair, with a red-and-blue striped t-shirt. He was barefoot.

"Welcome. Come see my palace. I hope my directions were easy to follow. I don't give out this address to just any Annie I meet at the Fair, you know." He led me into a construction zone. "Watch your step."

Roger and I had built our house, so I was familiar with the chaos of a building project. I liked it; it held promise.

Len stepped over boards lying in a neat pile on the floor. "Those will be framing this doorway." He took me through the house, his hand lightly on my back, steering me ahead of him. "I'll explain all this to you later. Right now let's go out to the back deck."

I followed him, going by an open closet, its door waiting to be hung.

From within the closet a glint of gold caught my eye, stopped me. A tall, wood-framed glass case was propped inside. Within the case a jacket was pinned for display. The material was of a translucent gold sheen. Looking closer I knew it wasn't cloth. It was constructed of long, foot-wide strips, had wrist length sleeves, and a hood, with laces. I'd never seen anything like it. Why was it in a frame? I called to Len.

"What's what?"

He backtracked. "Oh, that. I keep meaning to do something with it. Kinda neat, huh?"

"Is it a coat? What's it made of?"

He lifted the frame with both hands. "Here, you'll want to see this in the light. It is amazing." He carried it onto the back deck, where he propped it up against the railing. The slough beyond the deck was surrounded by tule and cattails with yellow-flag iris lining the edges. The air was warm and heavy with the early heat of the day. A light breeze moved across the porch.

I knelt to look at the coat. "What in the heck is this made of?"

His breath was warm on my neck as he moved close. "Gut from a seal. Opened up, and cut lengthwise, then sewed together. You really don't know what this is?"

He could be so superior, I'd forgotten that. "Uh, no."

He leaned back against the railing, looking down at me as he instructed. I stood up too.

"It's a Kamleika. Some people call them Aanoraks, but Kamleika is the native name."

"Native?"

"Inuit. You know, Eskimo."

"Oh, sure." Like I knew that. "And it is?"

"A jacket made to go to the Bering Sea. See how small the stitches are? This is life and death stitching." With his finger he followed one of the seams.

I leaned in closer, and felt his hand on my back.

He took it away to lift the frame. "But we can talk about this later. Not good for this to be out in the sun too long. Don't go away, I'll be right back."

While he was taking the coat back into the house, I watched birds chase insects over the vegetation, saw an occasional blue dragonfly setting itself on the railing. When Len returned, he brought me a glass of mixed cranberry and orange juice, with ice. We sat companionably in his Adirondack chairs, watching the action of the slough, insects flying and birds chasing.

"In mid-summer the mosquitoes made sitting out here impossible, but luckily for us, they've backed off now. Damn bloodsuckers. Or the birds ate them all. Good birds!"

Suddenly he stood and came behind my chair. He leaned over and rested his hands on my shoulders. "You know, you look dammed good. All my dreams about you didn't half measure up to the reality. You are one sexy broad."

My pulse picked up. He moved his thumbs onto my shoulder blades with a light massaging motion.

I leaned back onto his hands. He bent down, kissed the top of my head, and then moved quickly around my chair, where he took my hands to pull me up. Just like that we moved into our first kiss in thirty years.

I fell into the deep well of him, a warm tunnel that opened my heart. I adjusted my stance to fit closer against his body, my pelvis to press against his. I shifted my arms tighter around his back.

Eventually I pulled my lips from his, holding to our embrace but releasing my grip, clutching his biceps, wobbly on my feet. "Whew!"

"Here, follow me," he whispered.

He led me through the rooms again, dodging lumber on the floor, to a sunroom on the other side of the house. We sank together to the mat on the floor, sat facing each other, our legs entwined.

He took off my sandals, then my socks. He was already barefooted. I wiggled my toes against his, playing, and leaned forward for another kiss. As his lips met mine I experienced again that sensation of sinking into him, a delicious feeling.

Somewhere I heard a clock chime one-thirty. Where had the time gone? My body was completely in synch with uniting on the mat. It was hard to stop him as his hands stroked my shoulders again, but this time moving over my chest, going lower. I didn't want to stop.

I was out of time.

"Sam!" I grabbed Len's hands, wanting one more stroke. "I've got to get back and pick him up."

"Right now? C'mon! Just a few more minutes." He tried to twist his hands free. The old Len, no patience.

"Not enough time." I laughed, took a shaky breath. "For you, maybe, but not for me."

Bless him, he let his hands drop, reluctantly. "You're right. Tonight?"

I shook my head.

He groaned. "Let me know when you've taken your uncle home. We could meet in Cannon Beach?" He stood and grabbed my hands to pull me up. "I could rent a cabin. I've got the money if you've got the time."

"Oh, that would be too complicated. I'd like to come back here, or you could come to my place and I'll make dinner. Early next week?"

"Sounds good to me. Wine and candles? I'll bring the wine."

"That works for me. But, leave out the wine. Sparkling cider, please. I'll call you." I sat in a straight-backed chair and put on my socks and sandals, while my body still pulsed at what might have been. He pulled me up close, kissed the space between my breasts.

"Yum."

"I think a cool-down shower would be good right now," I said as he licked my neck. My nipples were hard against my sweater, aching.

He ran his hands, slowly, over them, lingering. It didn't help.

"Now?"

"No," I groaned. "For you. I'm leaving. I'm late as it is." One, last, kiss, his tongue wrapping mine. We pulled apart. I grabbed my purse and pulled out my keys, while heading for the door.

From the porch he watched me go.

I shut my car door and took a deep breath to steady my hand before I inserted the key. I didn't want to run over a curb with him watching. By the time I picked up Sam, I'd cooled down. But the memory stayed with me for the next few days, as if his fingers had left imprints on all my nerve ends.

I wanted more.

Chapter 15

A Short Stop

We spent Friday through Sunday of Labor Day weekend working around my place. Sam worked on the ship model and spent relaxing time at the picnic table with hot tea, watching the Clackamas swirl by, and talking to Magda on his cell. I harvested early produce from the garden, much of the time thinking of Len. I put my frozen chicken stock together with the veggies and fresh herbs, and made a dang good soup, for which Sam whipped up biscuits.

Late at night, when I couldn't sleep I went to what I now thought of as the Project Room. Sam had the ship parts laid out on a table with glue and paint and small brushes. I had Sophie's quilt on the larger table Roger had used. I moved my cloth pieces around.

Sophie's design wasn't working for me. I'd gone through my own small fabric stash, found nothing that would do for what I was thinking. The design need to be livened up, modernized.

The cat, Prince Charming, was as happy with Sam's company as I'd thought he'd be. Outside he helped us, walking the edges of the raised beds as I picked green beans and tomatoes. He inspected them in my basket. Inside, he sat beside Sam as he slowly put the ship together. He was also attentive as Sam talked on the phone to Magda.

I had two cords of wood delivered that Sam and I put away in the woodshed. We didn't need a fire yet, but I wanted to be ready.

On Labor Day I took Sam home, leaving early. We swung by Willamina to have breakfast with Magda at one of the old time restaurants. When we got out of our cars and hugged, Magda ran her hand down Sam's back.

Magda and Sam sat across from me, beside each other. While they were catching up I looked around at the place. It was vintage. The walls were hung with log-town ephemera: long saw blades used by two men to saw through the trunks of the enormous old growth trees, now sidelined and painted with scenes of lakes and trees under blue skies; photos of logging trucks loaded with one huge log, or at the most, three. Logs that if off center could tilt the truck, loads that if seen today would cause a traffic jam, and an environmental pile-up.

While we waited for service, Sam was trying to talk Magda into dropping everything and coming with us. "I can put you in one of Sophie's Cabins, introduce you around. Take you to the store where they sell material."

I figured that would get a reaction, not sure whether he did it on purpose or not. He does like to push at people's edges.

The menu was aged and a little spotted, with white tape over the prices, new amount written on the tape. The waitress was dressed in a sensible, just below the knee, slightly flared, brown skirt with a short apron over that. A button with her name, Edna, was pinned to her pale yellow blouse. She was carrying a coffee pot.

"Morning, Magda, I never see you this early. Anybody want coffee?"

"Had to bring in a couple out-of-towners to have a good breakfast. Yes, coffee please. What's good today?"

Edna recommended the travelers special, corned beef hash with over-easy eggs, coffee, $6.95. We all ordered it, Madga and Sam with a side of bacon. When she left, Magda elbowed Sam, "Remember, it's fabric."

I saw "gotcha" in his eyes. "So, how's Lena?" I said.

"Probably sleeping, but we'll meet today for the Quilt Guild. Have to have a short business meeting. Get everything nailed down for the Quilt Show. Sammy, you gotta come and see it."

With that she was back focused on Sam. I ate my breakfast and felt the coffee kicking in the energy for the rest of the drive. As I ate I thought about Len. I had my camera with me so, to redirect my mind I took a couple photos of the interior of the restaurant, of the glass eyes of the several stuffed deer heads and the hide of a black bear decorating one wall.

I was ready to be on our way, and finally, so was Sam. He hadn't been able to sidetrack Magda from her Guild duties. Near the old time cash register was a rack of postcards. I pulled out one showing a yellow dog walking down the empty main street of Willamina. "Wish You Were Here" was stamped across the bottom. I bought a couple.

"What do you want with those?" Sam said.

Magda bumped him with her shoulder. "It helps the local economy. Buy away, I say."

"Women." He patted his shoulder like she'd hurt him, causing us to glare at him. "Don't get me wrong. I love you all. Just can't say I understand buying junk you don't need."

"Hey, I might have to send you a birthday card someday." We said goodbye to Magda at our cars. Sam gave her a peck on the cheek as he helped her into her car. I promised to be back mid-week to work on the quilt with her.

Chapter 16

To The Beach

From Willamina I drove us to the coast, turning right above Lincoln City onto 101. Sam rolled down his window to feel the cool breeze off the ocean. The coast road took us through several small towns, swinging into Tillamook, then back through the coastal pine forests lining both sides of the road, some inland, some of it nearly hugging the waterline. I enjoyed the view of the waves splashing white on the beach, with people along the way playing in the surf, walking their dogs, or looking for agates.

To Sam this was going home, to me, a treat. September, the best time of year.

After about two hours I turned off 101, dropping down onto the road that ran through the small town of Cannon Beach. I was amazed as always at the traffic. When I was a kid the ocean had been more visible from the street. We could hear the waves rolling onto the shore, feel the mist on our faces. Now cabins, shops and restaurants all but hide the blue of the sea, offering only a tantalizing glimpse of the water.

I commented on the increase of buildings and people.

Sam said, "Nothing new about that. Everybody wants to come here. That's how Sue and I made a living, and how we...

well, Dave and Teri still bring in a few bucks. Have to admit, I don't quite get it. I'd rather go up the coast to a town that doesn't have hundreds of people trying to get into the same restaurant that I am."

"Maybe it's Ecola Park and Haystack Rock? Lewis and Clark walked here. Indian people fished and hunted here. Sam, it's a beautiful place. You're jaded, living in paradise your whole life."

"It was paradise when I was a kid, but in case you've not noticed, that was a long time ago. One of the good things about this place, I met Magda here among the thousands. She is special."

That made me wonder a bit but I knew that Sam and Sue had been a solid team, with no hint ever of the what he called, "Sheenagans," his rare reference to the situation of his birth. Of his father, David, impregnating a woman, Sophie, who wasn't his wife. Of Sophie and Sam, living with them, here, before she moved away, leaving Sam behind. His childhood had been different, that I had to give him.

He carried on a running commentary on the town as we drove through, remarking on what was new, which often meant it had come in thirty years ago. When locals hollered at him, "'Bout time you got back!" he waved back. I could tell he liked the attention.

We arrived at the old family house around noon. Teri had a lunch of tacos and salad ready. We hugged and she told me to make myself at home. "You'll be upstairs, in the guest room. Sophie's room." They had added a master bedroom and bath to the bottom floor and put a bathroom upstairs, with a railing by the steps, the only clue of changes needed for Sam. His room was now what had originally been David and Amy's bedroom. I settled into the room next door. It had wide board walls with simple hooks in a corner instead of a closet.

I opened my suitcase to retrieve the lightweight wool Pendleton shirt that I'd use for a jacket while I was here. Even though the days are still warm, the nights cool rapidly, a taste of the coming winter. The soft wind carries a bite.

I hung my jacket from one of the hooks. With that I felt at home looking out the same window that Sophie had over eighty years ago, onto the beach and Haystack Rock with its two sentinels. Her original cabin, down the slope, is still there, but so remodeled that it is nearly new. Right beside it are the five cabins that Sam and Sue built. Small cabins, each with a living room window view of the Rock. "Dramatic" they called it in their brochures.

After lunch Teri refused my help to clean up. "You go on down. The tide is perfect, still going out. When you get back you can take a nap." In my room I put on my jacket, dumped my binoculars into my small backpack and shrugged it on.

The path to the beach was straight on down the wooden steps David had built to accommodate the pitch of the short bluff. My feet hit the sand and I was in my own world. I sat on a log to take off my shoes and socks, and snugged them up to the driftwood, trusting that no one would steal my stuff here. They never have. I sat for a couple of minutes, squinching my toes in the dry sand, breathing in the air that is different, tangy with salt and the smell of sea creatures. I thrust myself off the log, trudging through the dry sand until finally it became damp and firm, much easier to walk on. My destination: The Rock. It was, as always, farther out than it looks.

Slick, lichen-covered rocks dotted the water. A family was spread out around the tide pools that encircled the base, mom and dad with their pants legs rolled up, two girls and a boy in shorts. The children were playing in the tide pools, splashing warm water at each other. They bent to the anemones that look like pretty purple flowers, touching the soft tubes that surround their mouths. When the tubes closed on their fingers, they pulled their hands away, and then poked them again, their mother admonishing them to, "Be careful. Remember, they're alive."

A perfect photo. I zoomed onto the face of one of the boys, showing his eyes round with wonder. I also caught the look of irritation as his mother cautioned him.

"Okay, okay."

Sharp barks came from a black and white Border Collie busy trying to round up the gulls. He was jumping as they flew just ahead of him, landing far enough away for safety but close enough to tease. The dog's pleasure made me temporarily long for a dog. Maybe a red setter running down the beach, fur flowing gracefully. Nothing like a dog at the beach. Now there'd be a business to have: Rent a Dog For a Day.

Shuffling my toes through the pools, I walked south to where the waves washed the shore along the tide line, the edge of the water curling into lacy patterns. Len crowded out all other thoughts from my mind, and I felt my internal body temp rising. The lace broke into ripples over my ankles, cooling me down. At the same time I relished my amorous feelings. I'd wondered if I was dead to love, if it was behind me.

The farther down the beach I went, the fewer people there were. I released myself to the happiness of this heaven, this perfect weather. When I looked down and saw a complete sand dollar, I picked it up, wrapped it in a hankie and put it in my backpack.

In the distance I heard yips from the dog and was startled to feel tears rolling down my cheeks.

What the heck?

Mom and Dad. Kids. A dog.

Yes, I'd wanted that. For myself, to be The Mom. For Roger to be The Dad.

I let myself swim in self-pity for a few steps, and then shook it off, pulled off the pack and rummaged for the binoculars. I lifted the glasses to my eyes and searched for Tillamook Rock Lighthouse—Aunt Sophie knew it as Terrible Tillie—just about two miles out. The rock is still there, with the building, but the light that Aunt Sophie took comfort from, no longer shines.

Thinking of Aunt Sophie and her lesson to me to enjoy life as it is and not waste time agonizing over unfilled desire, calmed me.

With the back of my sandy hand I wiped my tears, wishing I'd not used the hankie on the shell, and did the old trick of listing ten benefits in my life, The Gratitude List. My health, my eyesight, my fingers & toes—was I going to count them as ten, or one? That I can feel the water on my toes. That I'm at the beach. That I have Sam and Dave and Teri, and that they love me. And that I can love them. That's eight. That I have a house and that I have a place I can go take a nap, now, and be with family.

Enough. I turned around, taking into myself the roll of sea onto the sand, gulls hopping and squalling. Haystack Rock. A glorious place and a glorious day. The walk back was over too quick. A light fog was moving in, bringing that feeling of enclosure, with it the small damp. I found the log and shoes and socks where I'd expected them to be. I brushed my sandy feet, cleaned the grit from between my toes. The pleasure of the warm, dry socks comforted my cold feet.

Grateful for more than ten. I laughed to myself. More than eleven!

My nap that afternoon righted me, as did the evening meal of spaghetti and meatballs with salad and garlic bread. When we were all satisfyingly well fed, Teri stood and said, "Connor, help me with this. Hand me the dishes, I'll load the dishwasher and you can set out the cobbler."

Pleased to see how quick he was to help his mom, as if the promise of cobbler inspired him, I asked Connor how his bugs were doing. He was good at talking while moving, a family trait. "Everybody liked 'em. That picture you took with the cages shut tight, it was in our paper. It helped. They put my blue ribbon in the case at school, where the trophies are for the football guys."

Sam broke into a 1930's song. "We're in the money..."

Connor looked annoyed but laughed. "My little hisser guys are small but just as mighty as line backers when it comes to moving people. Wow, that was a tromp, wasn't it!?" When he had the table cleared, Teri handed him a casserole dish of blackberry cobbler, still warm, and me a spatula and a pile of bowls. Dave got a container of vanilla ice cream and a scooper. Connor handed spoons and forks around.

Sam sat waiting, spoon in one hand, fork in the other, anticipation deepening the wrinkles in his face. I ladled the cobbler into the bowls and Dave piled on the ice cream.

I said, "Sammy, you don't have to do anything but eat, huh?"

"Just who do you think picked these berries while you were messing around on the beach?"

"The family that works together stays together." Dave scooped ice cream on cobbler for Teri. Nobody commented on me calling him "Sammy". Maybe that was common here.

"Gramps, you did a good job. Man, oh man, this is good!

Mom, you make the best cobbler."

Sam sang out, "We're in the money..." drawing out the final word, "nowwwww," to which Conner nodded in agreement.

"Tell her about the aftermath of the bug stomp," said Teri.

"Oh, yeah! A couple days later that guy from the Salem paper came over, you know, the guy who took that photo. Said he knew you, that you guys are old friends. Fishing for info about you. Dad didn't tell him much."

Dave was nearing the end of his cobbler. "He talked about Grandma Sophie like you all was good friends. Said he was going to meet up with you. Has he done that yet?" His left eyebrow lifted in a question.

"Oh, yeah. He's sniffing around," Sam said. "She went to his house to meet up with him when I stopped in to see Kit."

"Sam! If Annie wants to see him you don't need to be saying stuff."

I knew my face was warming up. The memory of our hour set me into motion. I started taking dishes into the kitchen. With my back to them I could talk.

"His name is Len." All I could think was, *just pass this off like it's nothing.* "He's coming for dinner this week." Sam already knew that so it was better to get it out before he put his spin on it. Bad enough to have the family discussing my potential love life. "We were an item, once, but now we're just old friends."

I rinsed the bowls before putting them in the dishwasher. *Boy, I bet Sam's other mom, Amy, would have liked this feature.* To change subject I said to Connor, "Say, don't you have a board for Chinese Checkers around here somewhere? I think I won the last time we all played. Bet I can still beat you."

That did the trick. Dave cleared the table, Connor found

the board, and Teri pulled the old box of marbles out from where she'd kept them hidden from Connor and his friends when they were little and where it was still her secret.

The games came out even. We all won one, Connor two. We ended the evening with everybody happy. As I undressed for bed that night, I realized I'd decided. Len was back in my life for some reason. It was time I let loose of the chains I'd wrapped so tight around my heart, time to take a chance with feelings. I could always put my guard back up if it didn't work. The decision, along with the joy of family, led to an easy sleep.

I enjoyed my solitary ride back to the valley, though I dreaded returning to the heat. I used the time to think about the changes in my life over the last two weeks.

Quilting?

A romance?

Sam and Magda?

The Willamina show?

My life had been slow before the fair. Since the Bug Disaster it felt out of control.

At home I emptied my back pack, shook the sand from the shell, and set it on the windowsill in the kitchen.

Chapter 17

I Make a Move

Tuesday morning: I sat at my kitchen table, with early dawn outlining the bushes beyond the window. The sun was just coming up. I watched it through the trees, backlighting the far side of the river. The wind was gentle but with enough lift to raise branches of the maples. The early light cast shadows on the buttercup yellow of the kitchen wall. I thought about Len. I'd promised him dinner, and something more. The thought of more made me sit straighter in my chair.

The routine of making coffee soothed me. From the shelf above the sink I pulled down my favorite cookbook, a church cookbook. Some pages were spotty with grease. The book opened automatically to those recipes. Coffee ready I filled a mug, took it and the book to the table. The shadows had moved higher on the wall and continued to be tossed about.

I wanted to make something simple that I could pull from the oven, that would fill the house with good cooking smells. Not fish. Some onions, carrots, celery, potatoes, maybe a beet for more color. I had enough of the root veggies from my garden. A sponge cake with raspberry sauce I made from my patch. I looked at the photos of a lovely pot roast, thought about stuffed zucchini, and decided on simple. Steak. Baked potatoes. Asparagus. He would bring the drinks.

I rummaged in the bread bin, pulled out the leftover top and bottom heels of a loaf I bought last week before I took Sam home. I made toast, took it and peanut butter to the table.

Why Len, now? Was I looking forward to reuniting with a lost love?

Len had never been a true love to me, he had been more of a fascination. His moves had charmed me, but Aunt Sophie had thought he was dangerous. She had told me the story of her love affair to warn me of the dangers of fascination.

Perhaps fascination is just lust dressed up.

I finished up breakfast with a banana, cleaned up the crumbs from my peanut butter and toast, gulped the last of my coffee. I had shopping to do. And a phone call to make.

Chapter 18

Back at the Quilt Studio

I called Len and told him we were on for dinner Wednesday evening, early if he didn't mind. My plan was to have leisurely time to watch the sun go down while we ate, *et cetera*. He was quite agreeable, teasing again about the wine, "Are you sure you want sparkling cider?"

I went shopping, found a couple of nice steaks, had the cookbook out, reconsidered making a sponge cake from scratch, and was checking my linen closet when my cell rang.

What happened next made me think that Willamina has some similarities to Mayberry, both being small towns with bare-boned law enforcement systems.

I expected the call to be Len with more of his joshing, but Magda wailed into my ear, "Oh, Annie! It's awful! Please, can you come?"

"What? Magda, what's the matter?"

"Tommy! He's been here all the time. Come, please!" Her voice escalated in volume, causing my cell to vibrate. She sounded desperate.

I held it from my ear. "Tommy? Come where?"

"To my place. To the studio. Oh, God. The bear. We thought

he was here to scarf up apples."

She gasped. I heard another woman say, "Take a breath, ma'am."

Which I heard Magda do, while I went through a mental checklist. I'd need gas. I'd not unpacked from the Cannon Beach trip. Just throw the bag in the car, get gas, and go. Why not ask Sausage Roll Lena for help, I wondered.

As if she was listening to me think Magda said, "They took Lena to the hospital. She was having trouble breathing. One of the deputies said something about jail." This last bit came out again in the wail.

"Jail? Lena? Why would Lena go to jail?" While I was asking questions, I was dragging my bag from where I'd plunked it down when I came home. I put my cell on speaker phone while I took out the dirties, replaced them with clean underwear, socks and a couple t-shirts.

Magda kept talking while I moved around the room. "Lena. Me. I don't know. And Tommy's here. Uggghh!" This last sounded as if she had dropped the phone and was retching.

A man came on the line. "Ma'am, if you're a friend of hers you should come right away. We need help here. The body in the backyard has got to be taken care of. The dead bear, too."

Oh, my.

"I'll be there as soon as I can." For a millisecond I thought to get Roger, but then I remembered and damned him for not being here. I told the man—a cop?—to tell Magda I'd be there as soon as I could, and hung up.

Sam. I sat down on the bed and called him. He answered within a couple rings. Irrationally I thanked Roger for helping me. Who knows?

"Sam, Magda needs you." I gave him a quick rundown on

what I knew—not much—and what I planned to do. "When I get there I'll call you on my cell and you can talk to her. By then I'll know what's going on."

"Damn! I wish I had a car!"

I reminded him that he doesn't have a license anymore.

"So?"

I have to laugh. "Okay, Sam. I'll call you in a couple hours, maybe sooner."

"Thanks for letting me know. I'll wait a few minutes and call her myself. I want to know what's happened."

About to hang up I added, "Thanks, Sam." And felt another tiny pang for thanking him while resenting Roger for dying early. I get so tired of these conflicting feelings.

"Think nothing of it."

The trip seemed to take forever, but really took only about two hours. I spent the time re-running our conversation, trying to come up with a reasonable scenario to explain Magda's frantic call.

When I arrived I had to park alongside the road because the driveway was full of police cars, one that had *Sheriff* marked on the side. An ambulance was close in to the side yard.

Magda burst out of the house, followed by a policewoman with her arms out, like she had been restraining her and Magda had broken free. Her hair was sticking up all over, her eyes were wide and wild.

I was barely out of the car when she threw her arms around me.

"A-a-a-nnie, Tommy's here, been here all the time. In the backyard. Bear found him. They think I killed him. Please help me!" Her shriek scaled down to a whisper and I felt her grip lessening as she began to slip to the ground.

The woman, whose name tag identified her as Deputy Sheriff Avis Bybee, stepped forward and the two of us half walked, half carried Magda into the front room couch. With her head in her hands, she gave way to sobs. I put my arm around her and the deputy supported her on the other side. She said, "Mrs. Buler was just fine until you drove up, when she went crazy again. Maybe too fine."

A man in uniform came in and handed Magda a cup of water. She seemed barely aware as she sipped at it, but slowly her sobs stopped and she took several deep breaths.

She looked up. "Wish, you know I didn't do this." Apparently she knew this man whose name tag identified him as Sheriff Aloysius Kelly.

"Magda, there are certain procedures we must follow. It would be helpful to me if Deputy Bybee goes through what she knows. I'm sorry I couldn't get here before now. Take another drink there, Mag."

Deputy Bybee stood up and said, "Mrs. Buler here was working on her quilt. The other woman—Lena—went into the kitchen to get something. From the window by the sink, she saw a bear digging at the ground. She had a rifle in her pickup and went and got it. She came back through the house, past Mrs. Buler here, opened the back door and shot that bear dead. Before they realized what the bear had been digging up, Mrs. Buler called 911.

"Good thing, too, as it had been digging at the body of her husband. They both were screaming by the time we got here."

"Her husband? The bear killed him?"

"No. The bear was digging up Mr. Buler. He's been dead for some time."

"In the backyard?" To Magda I said, "I thought your

husband was away. Fishing? Somewhere on a boat?"

She sat up straighter and set the cup down. "I thought so, too. But I was wrong. And they think I killed him. Buried him here."

Tears streamed down her face. Deputy Bybee went to the bathroom and brought back a wet washcloth. Magda wiped her face with it, and her ragged breath calmed.

She worried at the cloth, said clearly, "I don't know how Tom got there, but I didn't do anything to him. Do you think that I'd have come here every day if I knew he was...out there?" She ran her hand over her head, pulling at her hair—easy to see how she got her scattered look. "Lord a'mighty." She sank back onto the couch, wiping at new tears.

"Where is Lena?" I said.

"Oh, that damn woman got hysterical when they took her gun away from her. So they carted her off. Yah, where's Lena? What did you do with her?"

"Your friend..." The Deputy pulled out a notebook.

"...was taken to the hospital first to be checked out, make sure she wasn't about to have a heart attack. I think they gave her a mild sedative to calm her down. She didn't have to be so hysterical. Not her husband. Then to the jail in McMinnville, where she is now."

"The jail?" Magda started up from the couch. The full import was penetrating her shock.

"Oh, she's all right." said Deputy Bybee. When I opened my mouth to protest her tone, she said, "Sorry. It's just that she caused a lot of trouble, shooting that bear. It's against the law to shoot inside city limits. Hope she's got a license to hunt bear. Out of season, anyway." An unexpected grin took the edge off her words. She flipped the notebook shut.

"You'd'a shot him, too! Did you see what he was into?" Magda's hand went to her mouth and the tears started again. She dabbed at them with the washcloth.

"Sure, I saw. What do you think we're doing here? We've taken a zillion pictures, lots of notes. Making a record. Called the Tribe at Grande Ronde to come salvage the remains of the bear." She turned back to questioning Magda. "I do wonder why your friend was so hysterical. Most likely they'll just book and release her. I'll see." She flipped her cell open and walked out the front door to the little porch.

While she was gone Magda put her hands on mine. "Do you think you could call Sam? Could he come? I don't know where my cell is."

He must not have been able to get through. "Sure, I'll call him in a few minutes. I suppose I could go get him if you want him here." No need to tell her I'm ahead of her on this. The look of relief on her face told me what I needed to know.

Almost.

I, too, wondered at Lena's hysteria.

I took the washcloth from Magda into the bathroom, refreshed it and myself, and took it back to her. She was slumped, alone, except for Deputy Bybee. She sat up and her eyes asked a question.

"I'll go call him now. And then take you home?"

Deputy Bybee said, "I don't think Mrs. Buler will be going anywhere right soon."

Oh.

Magda flashed me the first smile I'd seen from her. Not a real smile, closer to a grimace, but she was at least trying to surface from this nightmare. I bet she just wanted to go get a needle and stick it in some cloth, for the relief.

I arranged with Sam to pick him up the next morning, and then went back into the studio. "Any coffee around this place?" Magda started to get up but I put my hand out. "That's all right. I'll go make some in a while. First, we must figure out what's going on here."

"It's a mess, Annie. A real mess."

She had that right. I left her with Deputy Bybee, and went outside to call Len.

Chapter 19

Moving Tom

After I left Len a message to call me back, the sheriff suggested I take Magda home.

"We'll call when we need you," he said to her. "You are what we call, 'a person of interest'. I could detain you, but no need. I know where you live."

That was where I learned about Tom.

We sat at the table in the dining nook, to a dinner of canned soup and sandwiches I'd made with what I found in her cupboards and fridge. She was in mental shock.

"Tommy's drinking just turned everything to mush between us. Once he hurt me and I called Wish. Well, I called the sheriff and Wish came. After that, Tommy and I didn't trust each other. His words smashed all my feelings for him. He beat me down until I got to a point where I hoped he would die. Finally, it became unbearable."

Magda had been eating automatically, but with those words she put down her spoon. "His drinking dominated our lives. He became someone I didn't know and didn't want to have around. He was always into some scheme or other to make money, and he decided he wanted to be a commercial fisherman. I liked the idea. Maybe he would die at sea, or even better, make some money.

"He needed a boat to go fishing when and where and for as long as he wanted. And I wanted that too, for me. It was freedom, of a sort.

"We saved and borrowed, put every bit of cash into getting him a boat. Meantime he worked on other boats, to make money towards buying his own, learning what he needed to make a living at it."

"It?"

"Being a commercial fisherman. What to fish for, when, and where. How to store fish on the boat, what prices to expect for what fish. All the basics of taking care of a boat. It always needs work. That part was good for him. With his temper he had a hard time keeping a crew. Had to do most of the work himself."

"So, he makes a living fishing, now?"

She looked at me. "Not now."

Embarrassed, I took a look around. The house didn't feel like a fisherman's. There wasn't an old rowboat in the side yard or fishing gear lying around. Quilts and surfing equipment decorated her walls. In a corner was a large shelf with old lady stuff, knick knacks, little china chicks, a couple cows.

The surfboards intrigued me. Three of them hung from large hooks on the wall.

She smiled when I asked if Tom surfed. "Sure, he taught me how. We spent a lot of time at the beach. One of those boards is his. Two are mine. I was pretty good on a board. That was some years, and several pounds, ago. We loved doing that together, looking for that gift from the ocean, the curling roll of the perfect wave."

That set me to thinking about Roger and I, and Len and how I always seemed to be putting off our reunion. Was I waiting for a different wave?

I brought us back to now. "I wonder if they've taken him out of the back yard yet."

"Oh, God. Tommy's body. The sheriff said he needed to take photos of it in place and lift it carefully so's not to disturb any evidence that might show how it got there." Her lips turned down in despair. "I've been thinking and thinking. When was it I last heard from him? What'd he say? He was coming home, I know.

"Then he didn't." She lifted her tea mug, and then set it down without taking a drink. Distracted.

She rose from the chair so rapidly that it teetered.

I grabbed it, set it right.

"I gotta go back there!" Her eyes were wild again. "Will you go with me? Take me?"

"Sure. But calm down. Why do we need to go back there?"

"He's my husband. I want to know what happened. And if they took him to Treeline yet." Treeline was the local mortuary. "There are things to do."

My cell rang. The ID told me it was Sam. "Yo," I greeted him. "I'm here with Magda. We're going back to the studio. Here, you talk to her."

She took the phone with a huge sigh. "Oh, Sammy. I can't wait 'til you get here." She listened. "You can stay at my place. Not a motel." She gulped and I feared she was going to start wailing again, but no. She pulled herself together and said, calmly, "I need you here."

So easy for her to say. Did I feel that way about Len? Roger had been the right guy but he hadn't stuck around.

Magda had had the opposite problem. She couldn't get hers to stay away. Until now. I remembered seeing that in a poem once:

> Why do the ones we want
> to go,
> stay?
> And the ones we want
> to stay,
> go?

A good question.

We arrived just as they were lifting the body from the ground. Deputy Bybee led us through the house to the small cement patio. "Don't go any farther, you understand? Are you sure you want to be here?"

I wasn't, but Magda held her hand to her mouth and nodded. I'd hoped he would be gone to the morgue. An old quilt was wrapped around the body. It was tattered and torn. By the bear? Or time? *Ironic,* I thought, as even I recognized the pattern. *Wedding Ring.*

"It's him, all right," Magda whispered to herself.

The deputy looked at her curiously, because Magda had been so matter of fact.

"It's my husband and my house, I don't think it can get any worse, do you?"

Deputy Bybee rolled her eyes. "That remains to be seen."

"Frankly, I've seen about all the remains I can handle." I pushed down nausea as I made my way back into the kitchen. With a thump I sat onto a chair at the table where we'd all had pie just a few days ago. My cell rang just as I was digging it out to call Len. It was him.

"Sweetheart, how goes it?" His voice was full of concern.

I relaxed into the warmth of him, that side that was gentle, caring, and knew what to do. Forgetting my doubts I poured my troubles into his listening ear.

He cut to the chase. "I guess this means that tomorrow is off?" His tone was neutral.

"You don't mind?"

"*Au contraire*, my little chickadee, I mind a lot." His voice purred into my ear, which tingled as if his fingers had traced the rims, lightly, but with just that little bit of pressure that made me want more.

My mind raced, feeling for loopholes. "I am going to be busy tomorrow, going down to fetch Sam and bring him back. Say! Do you want to go with me? You know, I could really use your help in this."

"Sure, if you want me to. I've already cleared the decks for the day, so I'm free. How about I pick you up around... Wait, where should I pick you up? You staying with Magda tonight? In Willamina?"

Magda and I had talked it over and she had a friend who could come and stay with her tomorrow. Now that I thought of it, why shouldn't I take her along with Len and me to pick up Sam? That way, nobody could get in trouble.

It might help take her mind off the immediate work that would have to take place in the backyard. It was all quickly arranged.

Deputy Bybee said Magda could go with us to pick up Sam, but she made it clear to me that she didn't want Magda left alone. "I'm just worried about her state of mind. I know how I'd feel if we found my husband buried in my backyard."

"She's not a suspect?"

"Not on the face of it, no. I was there when she first saw

him, and I don't believe she suspected in any of this." She shrugged. "I could be wrong, but I'm good at what I do, and one of the things I do is trust my experience. Besides, I talked to my mom, who's known Mrs. Buler all her life and she says to look in a different direction. We have other clues." She put her hand on my shoulder, "Just watch her. She's highly thought of in this town, and that ain't no small potatoes."

Magda was ready to leave. She handed me a large cloth bag, homemade of course. "Here. Your quilt. We're gonna have some time on our hands. Let's be productive."

I was hoping she'd forgotten the quilt. The closer we got to doing it, the bigger the knot in my stomach became. Oddly, I took the bag with a feeling of serenity. "You have what we need at your house?"

"You betcha. I don't know much about murdering bears but I do know quilting. Ain't nothing like it to calm you down. You'll see."

I wondered if she was talking to me, or herself. No matter.

We left the people in the backyard to gathering clues and moving the body on out of there. Deputy Bybee watched us leave, with a last caution. "You leave your cells on. We'll be calling you when you can return here. Meanwhile, go on down to Cannon Beach. But, come right on back, okay. No time for funning around down there."

As we climbed into my car the officers were loading Tom's bagged body into the back of a van. Magda took one long look, gave a small nod, and moved on into the passenger seat. We were buckling up when she said, "I guess that's that, huh. I never thought it'd come to this."

"Did you ever think about how it might end?" Neither one of us questioned what "it" meant.

"I'm not surprised somebody offed him and buried him in the backyard. Just never imagined it would be my backyard."

We waited while the morgue people finished up with locking the double doors of the van. They backed out slowly, turned down the hill and moved on down the road. Taking the body to autopsy, not to Treeline Mortuary.

I gave the van some distance before I followed it down the road. Neither of us said a word..

It was barely dusk when we got back to her house, a cottage with a large trellis arched over the walkway to the front door, overgrown with a rose bush coming from each side and meeting in a tangle overhead. Thorns snagged my blouse and caught in my hair as we walked under it. The whole front looked shaggy, like no one was much paying attention to it.

I reminded myself to tell Sam to bring his garden tools. We had work for him to do. He was going to be one busy guy.

Chapter 20

A Hard Night

From my bed in the guest room I heard Magda cry out. Nightmares?

I turned on lights on the way to the kitchen where I drew a glass of water. Remembering Deputy Bybee's earlier kindness, I found washcloths in the bathroom cupboard, and soaked one with warm water. When I entered her room, she was sitting on the side of her bed, shaking. I turned on her bedside lamp and handed her the water.

She took a deep drink before handing it back to me. "Thank you." She buried her face in the comfort of the warm cloth while I sat beside her and put my arm around her shoulders.

"Annie, This is the most awful thing that has ever happened to me." She tossed her head. "Oh, listen to me. It's not about me. It happened to Tommy. And here I am, looking forward to a trip to the beach tomorrow to get Sammy. I'm a real piece of work, that's what I am."

She breathed a deep sigh. "I know what happened to Tommy is real, but in my dream it was just so sad, him sitting under the apple tree, saying, 'Are you happy? I'm gone for good, now.'" She took another drink.

"God forgive me, I'm not sorry he won't show up on my doorstep again. Drunk. Crazy. Whoever killed him did me a favor.

"Oh! I don't really mean that. It's just that it's been such a long time I've been afraid that he'd come back home. Never knowing. Looking over my shoulder, wondering if he was going to show up and wreck something."

She set the glass down and tugged at the bedding. I lifted the covers, and she pulled her legs and body back onto the bed. I plumped up her pillows and with a little groan she lay back down.

"Do you think you can go back to sleep now? If you don't sleep I wonder about you coming with me tomorrow. With Len and me," I amended, "to pick up Sam. We could always bring him to you."

"No. I'll be okay. I need the trip."

As I leaned to turn the bedside lamp off, I saw a twinkle, dim but lighting the corners of her eyes.

"Besides, someone has to chaperone you two. That boy is up to no good. You mark my words." The twinkle faded and I clicked off the light. "Thank you for helping me. Lena's a basket case and most of my friends are on a quilt retreat. I felt so alone."

"Glad to help," I whispered but I don't think she heard me, because the next noise from her bed was a light snore.

Chapter 21

Magda's Morning After

When I woke the morning after the bear found Tommy, I felt drugged. I lay there gathering my bearings until my body propelled me to the bathroom. I needed to scrub off everything that had happened yesterday. As I stood under the shower nozzle with the hottest water I could handle pouring over me, my head began to clear. The nightmare was over. Soaping up a washcloth, I washed Tommy's touch, from my face to my toes, down the drain. Yesterday had been the final straw in a lifetime of nightmares with him.

The Quilt Show was coming up and I had responsibilities.

Annie was moving around in the kitchen. I heard cupboards being opened and shut, then the smell of coffee. I prefer tea in the early morning but I was relieved to not have to make any decisions. Coffee would do fine. Annie's quilt needed finishing, and I needed to teach her how to do that. While I dressed I mentally put fabric together, laid out batting and put a backing on it. I imagined it about ready for CanDoIt, the name I'd given my quilting machine.

I pulled on tan pants and a pink sweater, the brown walking shoes I always take to the beach, and accessorized with shell earrings and a heart necklace.

Annie was buttering toast. "Coffee there for you, Magda, if you want it." She pointed to the cup at my place, with bowl and spoon. The tablecloth was one of my flowered pieces of fabric, a large square of thin cotton printed with roses of pink and red.

Tommy had sneered as he was readying to leave this last time. "I'll be glad to be rid of all this girlie cloth with little flowers."

I'd looked around after he left, and dang it, I did have lots of flowered fabric. I bought more but he never got to see it. I suppose that's for the best.

"I'll be glad," I'd snapped back, "when I don't have to listen to you sneering at me, either."

He'd been surprised when I said that. I usually just go quiet when he attacks my quilting.

I noticed what Annie was wearing. "Lord, girl, do you think that neckline's low enough?"

She tugged at the neckline of the dark blue sweater, trying to bring it up so not quite so much cleavage was showing.

"That doesn't help much. I like your skirt, love the way it sways, and florals are my favorite, but, a skirt to the beach?" I went into my room and brought her a camisole. "Save the boobs for him, I'd rather look at fabric." I threw it to her.

She sat down at the table and laid the lacy camisole in her lap. Took a sip of her coffee.

"That guy's got you in a tailspin," I said while I filled my bowl with Wheat Chex, poured on the milk, sprinkled on some sugar and ate with an appetite that surprised me.

Annie mumbled through a bite of toast, "Yeah. I guess."

I couldn't say that I was any better. I should have been thinking about Tommy and was wondering how Sammy would like me in pink? Were we crazy, or what?

Hormones. I'd thought I was done with that stuff, until Sammy and I stumbled back into each other's lives. I'd worried that I was in a pickle, being married and all, but now that problem's solved. Sorta, kinda.

I still couldn't figure out who'd killed him. I knew it wasn't me. Why was he in the back yard?

"He'll be here any minute. Thanks for this, I'll give it back to you."

For a minute I was confused, as I'd been thinking of Tommy. He? Oh, Len. "Just don't let him tear it off you!"

She laughed, dumped the last of her coffee into the sink and went into the guest room. A few minutes later she came out, wearing the camisole and carrying the sheets from her bed. "I'll put these in the washer. Where do you keep your clean sheets? You want the bed to be fresh for Sam."

I pointed to the linen closet just as the doorbell rang. Len. I let him in.

She was right behind me, clean sheets in hand. "Just in time to help me make a bed."

He is cute, especially when he smiles like that, though there is still something about him that puts me off.

"Glad to be of help." They went into the bedroom while I gave the kitchen a slapdash wash up.

"All ready!" When they came out, Annie's face had a soft glow that hadn't been there before.

Len patted my shoulder, said something about hanging in there, and opened the front door for us. "Beauty before age." He swept us out the door in front of him.

As I passed him I said, "You're a sweet talker, ain't you?"

He didn't answer, but smiled as he closed the door behind us.

Annie and I gasped together when we saw what was in the driveway.

Chapter 22

Retrieving Sampson

In the driveway was a classic powder-blue Thunderbird. four-door. Len stepped to the front passenger door "You called Madam? Your carriage awaits."

"Oh, Len. It's beautiful. I had no idea you had such a fantastic car." I trailed my hand against the light blue paint as I walked to the front to admire the classic Thunderbird logo stretched across the wide grill, the wings of the powerful icon balancing either side.

Len came up beside me, saying, as he put his hand on my shoulder, "Oh, this old thing?" He leaned close to whisper, "I do have my secrets," and nibbled ever so lightly on my ear.

Magda said, "Ahem!" right behind us. "Now, that's why I'm coming along." She stared at the car, finally said, "I should'a guessed you'd have a fancy rig to match your talk."

"Oh, Miz Magda, you say the sweetest things." He left me to my examination of the car and went to Magda, who was standing beside the rear door on the driver's side. He opened it, offering his hand to help her in.

She put her purse and coat into his hand and slid onto the black leather seat, going only halfway across. "I'll just stop

109

here so I can be close behind to help you with your driving."
She took her purse and coat, placing them beside her, and
buckled up. "Glad to see you've modernized her."

"Hey, of course. It's the law." He shut her door, gently, but
with a firm thrust.

I was at my door and reaching for the handle when he
called, "Wait a minute, I'll be right there." He crossed behind
me to grasp the handle and give it dramatic pull as he opened
it. Bowing slightly, he waved me in. "Miz Annie."

We followed the same road as I'd taken the week before,
but with more attention from other travelers. Len loved it,
raising a finger off the steering wheel in acknowledgement of
honks or waves. I think he was sorry we made such good time,
so much so that he passed up the first entrance into Cannon
Beach and drove the few miles to come into town from the
north end, allowing him to parade the T-bird back through
town.

We took the street that parallels the ocean. Shops lined
both sides, mostly old cottages with multipane windows and
flowerboxes, now converted into specialty stores, galleries,
or cozy restaurants. The dirt or gravel alleyways were red-
bricked over, each brick edged with green moss. Streetlamps
hung with flower baskets, pansies and nasturtiums flowing
over the edges. Attractive to people, but slow going for cars.
Our stately creep gave folks time to admire the car, and Len to
absorb the glory.

"I think this street is one of the most interesting in Oregon,
don't you?" I was surprised to see a smile on his face. His dark
eyes were large with happiness, unlike the frustration of most
people I'd ridden with here, caught up in this everlasting road
jam. The two-lane street was bordered with parked cars and
both lanes were moving slowly.

"I don't think I ever thought about it. It's always been this way." I said.

"No, not always." Magda said from the back seat. "In the old days there were few stores. These shops were cabins for rent. The streets were muddy and full of gravel from the side roads. But the town always did have traffic. When I first met Sammy it was crowded on the weekends, but not jammed up all summer, like now."

Ah, a chance to clear up something. I turned around. "So, when was that? When did you meet Sam?"

"Let me see. I was about thirty when I came down to stay with my friends at his cabins. That was thirty-seven years ago. Sam was fifty, thereabouts. And good looking, too, let me tell you. Those blue eyes and cute butt.

"He's still a good looking man. Lucky, too. Can still walk and talk, and think."

She's smitten. I'm happy for Sam.

We'd traveled the full length of Cannon Beach, past town now, to an easy turn-off to the beachside house.

Wider than the cabin Aunt Sophie had described to me, the house was now substantial, with a driveway to a garage where the chicken yard used to be. No lines out for washing. No outhouse. Modern, yet it holds the charm of an old place. Still an apple tree in the yard by the road. A small garden surrounded by a white picket fence in need of painting. But then, things on the coast almost always need painting.

We'd barely pulled into the yard when Sam came from behind the house, along the brick path. "Well, there you are. I thought you'd never get here. How late did you leave, anyway?"

Len got out of the car to shake his hand. "You never change, still giving fits after all these years."

"Len? For Gawd's sake, I'd'a thought you'd'a died of meanness by now. Where'd Annie pick you up?"

I came around the car to give him a hug. "We were hitchhiking down the highway and he picked us up. Didn't you meet Len at the Fair? He's the one took that photo of the bug stomp, the one on the front page of the Salem paper."

"Yeah. Helped us in the long run. We won the prize for exhibit that drew the most interest, the most visitors. All thanks to you. Glad to have you on our team."

They had only met a few times, the first being long ago when I'd taken Len to Sophie's Cabins while we were still dating, before I finally took Aunt Sophie's advice, and dumped him.

Len said, "I'm going to take a quick run on the beach while you two gather up 'Ol Sam, here. Okay?" He'd already reached into the car for his jacket.

"Teri's cooking up a bit of lunch for us, so don't be gone too long," Sam said. Len threw up an arm to show he'd heard, and went on. I watched him go between two of the cabins. The air had a light, damp mist. I breathed it in, loving the smell of brine and seaweed. Refreshing.

Magda stopped at the bathroom when we went inside.

To Sam I said, "Bring your work basket, the one with pruning shears and stuff to work on Magda's yard." I wasn't really sure how much Sam was capable of doing anymore but I know he's got the magic touch when it comes to anything with plants. I think he'd liked to have been a farmer. He has a degree in agriculture. Magda's yard would be a cinch for him.

"Good, I'm glad you thought of it. You know I like to get my hands dirty."

While he went into the garage I went through to the

kitchen. When Magda joined me, I introduced her to Teri, who was setting out an easy lunch of canned chili and hot dogs.

"Magda, I'm glad to meet you. Sorry it's under such not-so-good circumstances." She took Magda's hands in hers. "I'm sorry for your loss. Annie, there's some salad makings on the counter here. If you could mix that up we'll be about ready." She gave Magda's hands a good squeeze, and then let her go, and looked around. "When you called this morning I thought you said you were bringing your old beau. Len?"

"He's taking a quick run on the beach. When he gets back he can eat what's leftover." To stop any more talk about him, I said, "Will Dave and Connor be having lunch with us?"

She handed me the silverware and gave Magda a tray with a packet of buns, and bottles of hot dog fixings. "No, Dave's driving truck today and Connor is at school, so it's just us. I stayed home so I could see you and get Gramps off." I chopped tomatoes and lettuce and a cucumber and we were ready. Teri went to the garage door and hollered for Sam. "Hey, kid! Grub's on, better get in here if you want some."

Sam came in quickly, "I don't need to be called twice!" To me he said, "I've set my toolbox just outside the garage door. When Len comes back he can lift it into the trunk. I'm good at a lot of things but lifting that toolbox isn't one of them. Do me good to see him work."

At that we heard a knock on the door and Len opened it. "It's me."

"Come right on in," hollered Teri from the kitchen. "Everybody sit there at the table." She came out, handed the plated dogs to me, gave Magda a large bowl of chili with a serving spoon. While we took the food to the table, she went back to get a small bowl of chopped onions and a glass of buttermilk. "Anybody else want buttermilk? Gramps gotta have it."

"Helps with the heartburn," he said, and laughed.

Len had just come in after throwing his jacket on a bench by the door.

Teri said, "We've never met. I'm Teri, Dave's wife. Set yourself down, we don't stand on ceremony around here."

Which he did, in the chair by me.

He concocted his chili dog combo with relish, adding cheese and onions with abandon.

Sam made himself a chili dog, adding the onions sparingly, saying quietly, almost to himself, "Gosh, I love onions but they don't love me so much anymore." That was his second reference to advancing years, I wondered if he was feeling nervous about Magda, his younger woman.

I leaned across the table and whispered to him, "We have antacid in the car. Enjoy your lunch." He tucked in.

"I found an old quilt of Sophie's that she never finished. I wanted Magda to complete it for me but she's going to teach me how to do it."

"It's an interesting project and a good one for her to learn on. It will be a challenge."

Sam said, "And you could do with a distraction right now. Annie's a good one for that."

"How's that?" I asked.

"You're always learning something or going somewhere. You do stuff."

"I like to keep busy, keep my mind working. I think that's a good thing."

"Oh, no problem with it, just saying that you are the perfect person to help Magda right now."

Magda piped up, "Huh. I thought I was helping you."

Teri said, "This all has got to be terrible for you."

"Yeah." Magda sighed. "It's a mess. But Sammy here will be a help to me. I have to talk to the sheriff tomorrow, and then all the things to do with Tom's..."

I guess she couldn't bring herself to say "body".

She stopped and put down the hotdog. "I just can't figure it out. But tomorrow is another day. Everything will come to light in time. Tonight the guild women will be back from their retreat and they can help me sort everything out. Annie and I have that quilt to finish." She lapsed into silence.

Len had apparently been quiet long enough for him. "Miss Magda, don't you worry. We'll get this all worked out for you."

Sam said, with an edge to his voice, "Yes, we will. Soon's as you are done feeding your face you can put my tool box in the trunk and we can be on our way. You've had your run, so I guess you're refreshed enough now to get back on the road?"

Lord, what was the matter with him?

"Don't you worry about it, old man, I've got it under control." Len snapped back.

Men. For some reason these two had burrs under their saddles. Remembering Len's jealousy and assumed ownership of me in the past, I concluded that burr must be me, and that Sam was put off by Len's propriety behavior. Feeling protective of Magda, too? Roosters. It might be a long ride to Willamina. But then Len would take me home and we'd have dinner. Maybe that would soothe him. I was looking forward to a break from all this grief. Time enough to take it back up tomorrow morning when I return to Willamina to help Magda.

"We ought to get back. Magda, did you want to go down to the beach before we leave?"

"No, I can do without that. I'd like to take back some saltwater taffy, for the gals. Is there a candy store on our way out of town?"

Teri said, "I just happen to have a boatload of taffy. I'll give you a bag. All kind of flavors."

Magda added, "I do have one other thing I'd like to do, if we have time. And I don't know why we wouldn't. Nobody's waiting for me to show up. Except the cops. And they can wait."

We all laughed at her bravado.

"You have a great fabric store here in Cannon Beach. I'd like to stop there."

Len put down his spoon, said, "Capitol idea, Magda. I'd like to stop there myself. I need some backing for the quilt I'm making for my son."

I stared at him.

"What? You do remember that I quilt, don't you?"

"Yes, I guess so. Just didn't think of you shopping for material."

"Fabric, Annie dear." Magda stood and was starting to help clear the table.

Len finished his lunch and cleaned up his plate with his last bit of bun. He took his plate into the kitchen and set it on the counter. "Now, Sam, where'd you say that toolbox is? I'll get your stuff in the trunk and we had best be on our way. We've got a stop to make and that might take some time, if I know women, and shopping."

Magda shook her head. "No rush on my account."

Teri came from the pantry with a bag that she handed to Magda. "Your taffy."

Magda thanked her. We all went outside, where the men

were dealing with the tool box. I saw Len carrying it in a mock stagger, his back bent, his mouth twisted in an exaggerated grimace as he groaned under the weight of it.

Sam said, "Still a funny guy, huh? Bring it over here. Be careful not to strain yourself."

Len grinned and straightened to set the box down at the back of the car.

Sam said, "This is one heck of a car, Len. Nice lotta shiny chrome. The best part about it is the great trunk. If you would just lift the tool box into it, I'd be grateful. The part of my back that lifts doesn't work all that good, anymore."

"You probably threw it out when you packed this thing." Len hefted the box into the trunk. "Whatcha got in here, a body?"

We women were hugging goodbye. As one, we stopped and stared at him, Magda especially.

She shook her head at Len. "You're a case, you are."

Sam opened her door. She got in and Sam went around to the other side.

"Sorry. Wasn't thinking." Len put Sam's bag on top of the toolbox and closed the trunk. He turned to Teri and put out his hand. "Thanks for the lunch. Someday Annie and I will come down and stay in the cabins. We did that many years ago, you know."

"I've heard that. You are welcome anytime Annie brings you."

"Well. Thanks again." He got in the car, shut the door, and rolled down the window.

"Drive careful." Teri said.

"I will."

"We'll be back," Magda said.

I was turned around to help Len back out the driveway and saw Sam reach across the seat to her and take her hand in his. "Yes, we will," he said, and squeezed it.

"Next stop, the quilt shop," I said.

Chapter 23

Into a Fabric Store

The fabric store was a few blocks from the beach house. I'd barely adjusted to the pressure of the seat belt, when Len pulled into the driveway. From the backseat Magda said, "Yup, this is a good one. I've always come away with something I can't get anywhere else."

Len said, "Ever been in a bad fabric store, Magda?"

"Don't mess with me, boy, I'm feeling good, here." The click of her seatbelt announced she was moving out. "Good variety of buttons here."

"Do we need buttons?" I said, as I opened the door.

"No, not today, but they are fun to look at. And you never know when you might want to make a button quilt."

I don't want to make any kind of quilt, was all I could think, but I did wonder just what a button quilt would involve. "I think I have a glass jar of old buttons from Aunt Sophie's stash, if it ever comes to that." Just to let her know I was equipped with buttons.

"Hey, you're getting the lingo."

"From being around you." I laughed.

She was reaching for the door of the shop when Len

reached from behind me and opened it for both of us. Sam brought up the rear.

"Oh, smell that fabric," said Magda. I couldn't smell anything in particular, but my vision was filled with color. Bolt after bolt of fabric-lined narrow aisles from which to examine, drool, and exclaim.

"Yeah, there's a lot of material in here."

Her head snapped around.

Before she could correct me I said, "Gotcha. Just wanted to see if you were paying attention."

Sam wandered over to the button display. From the rack he pulled a packet of gray buttons with a bronze Celtic Cross on each one. "I think I remember some of these. My preacher Grandpa used them to button up his overalls when he worked in the garden."

"Oh, Sammy, you're just too funny." Magda went over and took them from his hand and slid the packet back onto the rack. "More likely you wore them back in the Dark Ages, to keep your knickers up."

They laughed together, softly.

She tilted her head at him and brushed a hand across his forehead, pushing back white locks that had fallen over his eyes. They looked and acted like a long-time, happily married couple.

Len was fingering a dark blue cotton with a random pattern of all-over sports equipment: footballs, baseballs, basketballs.

"Is that what you're looking for?"

"Almost, but not quite." He moved down the aisle to lightweight corduroy of autumn orange, with a repeat pattern of a football sailing between goal posts. "Ah, this is it. Bright enough for him to not lose it in the Laundromat. If he ever washes it." He took the bolt to the counter and said to the clerk, "May I leave this here until I'm done looking?"

The clerk, as too many women seemed to do, responded as if he'd personally offered her something. "Certainly. No trouble at all. I'll make a special pile here." She smiled at him. "That your 'Bird out there?"

"Sure is."

"1967?"

"You know your 'Birds."

"The doors tipped me off. My dad had a Thunderbird, a '57, red. Red outside and red and white inside. A convertible with short fins and porthole windows. The hardtop came off. Just two doors so we kids didn't often get to ride in it. He and Mom would whiz away in that thing. You buy it new?" She looked to be about thirty and it was clear that she wasn't flirting with him but with his car.

His lips closed in annoyance before he said, "Almost. That okay with you?"

"Sure, just meant you've taken real good care of it." She smoothed his feathers with another smile. "She doesn't look like she's had a bunch of owners."

She came from behind the counter and went over to Magda and Sam, "Can I help you?"

"I'm looking for a beach pattern. To back a quilt we're working on. Hey, Annie. Come see what's here."

I pulled myself away from Oriental prints with cranes on them.

"Magda, I had no idea. This is like a gallery."

"Don't get hung up there. You need to concentrate. Those Orientals are beautiful but won't work with what you're doing.

121

See this sandy design with little shells in it?"

I was near dizzy with the patterns and designs on the fabric bolts all over the store. "Magda, this could make me crazy."

"Focus here. Imagine it flipped back against the front. Will it complement? Clash? Not go at all? I don't know what you want. I can just give you my advice. And then you won't know if it really works until it's done."

I agreed with the sand and shells. She put it on the counter, next to Len's bolt.

"Now, I think that you're rather scarce on tools. Is that right?"

"Tools? For sewing? I have scissors and thread. What else do I need?"

"What kind of scissors?"

"Sewing scissors. They're good ones, inherited from Aunt Sophie with her sewing stuff."

"We'll get you some rotary scissors. You could borrow mine but you'll be needing them later."

"Rotary scissors? What in the heck are those?"

She directed me to a rack and selected an oblong case: "These." She handed the case to me.

"What later?"

"You'll be making other things." The clerk led us over to a table with an assortment of tools. Magda picked up a packet of long pins with flat, bright yellow heads and threw them in a basket. Added a saucer-like dish. "Great pin holder. It's magnetic. Keeps your pins from scattering to hell and gone when the cat jumps in the middle of them."

From a rack she pulled some flat, rectangular, plastic

things. "Rulers." They didn't look like rulers to me—different lengths and widths, see-through green with black markings on them. "You'll need a couple of these. Ah, mats." She added a hard rubber mat marked with a grid. It looked to be about thirty inches square.

"Now wait a minute. My aunt didn't need all this to make a quilt."

"You will be glad for each and every one of these things before we're done. Time savers. Table savers. This mat here is going to serve you in so many ways. You'll wonder how you ever worked without it."

"I get along."

She moved to the thread rack. "Some Invisible Thread. That's always handy."

I walked over and snatched it out of her hand. "'Invisible Thread'? I think not. This must be the joke section."

She laughed at me, but then frowned. "Oh, ye of little faith."

"Looks like fishing line to me. Why not just stop at the tackle shop and save some money?"

Len came over and lifted the spool from my fingers. "Ah, my sweet one, you have much to learn. Magda's right, these tools will make sewing fun. And the precision you will gain from these rulers and the mat make it worth your money. The rotary scissors will halve your cutting time." He picked up the oblong case that I'd put on my pile, and opened it to show me a sharp, round blade attached to a hard plastic handle. "Be extra careful with these. They're as sharp as an X-Acto knife." He closed the case and dropped it back in the basket.

Sam came over. "Are we about through here? I could go out and sit in your toy." He gave Len a look.

The clerk said, "Ready?" She checked out my purchases,

then went to attend to the bolts with Magda. She cut the length Magda asked for. When she picked up Len's bright autumn orange with footballs, she said, "If you ever want to get rid of that old car out there, I'd take it off your hands. You could buy something more to your style, racier, like a Mustang."

"You gonna pay me $30,000 for the 'Bird?"

"Naw. Not today. It's fun to see it, though. Reminds me of my younger days. Please stop in next time you are driving by. We'll see if a bundle of cash has dropped in my lap by then."

I stepped up and took his arm. Whether she was flirting with him or the car, I'd had enough of it. "We'll do that. In case we need any more fabric."

She pulled up the bolt, turning it to an angle easier to cut from, then let it fall to the table with a harder *thunk* than need be. "Whatever."

Magda was looking at me with a wry grin.

Sam said, "I think you've got everything you need. You've got all your tools, right?"

Embarrassed at my snappishness, I picked up my bag and said, "I'll see you in the car." My face was flaming.

Len handed me the keys.

I wasted no time going through the door. In the splendor of the T-Bird's black leather interior I thought about the scene I'd just caused. Couldn't blame the clerk, she was just responding to Len.

By the time they came out I was calmed down. I needed to get a grip on these feelings that swept through me whenever a woman flirted with Len. It wasn't his fault. Or was it?

We made it to Magda's in good time. Len carried Sam's toolbox into the garage. Magda had settled Sam into her guest room when we came in to say goodbye. "You sure you won't stay for dinner? I've got some stew I pulled out this morning from the freezer."

Len set down Sam's suitcase. "Thanks, Magda, but we've got dinner all planned. Annie's cooking for me and I'll help her."

"Always nice to work together," said Sam. "We'll see ya early tomorrow then, Annie?"

Before I could answer, Len said, "We'll be here as early as you need us. About ten?"

Magda was at the closet, sliding stored clothes aside to give Sam room. "Sure. I'll let you know if I need you any earlier. I 'spect I'll be seeing the police, and then I have some other details that must be attended to. Thanks for bringing Sam. You two have a good dinner."

We tried.

Chapter 24

A Variety of Conflicts

He started teasing the moment he opened the car door for me. "Finally, I'm going to give you the ride you've been asking for." He leaned down to kiss my cheek.

I turned so his lips met mine, in a quick pass. Smiling, he pulled back to shut the door.

I leaned across and lifted the inside handle to let him in his door.

"Thanks. I like that."

"You're welcome," I said. "We've been in the car seems like all day. I'm ready to be home."

"Me too." He buckled up, and then reached across to run his right hand over my hair, drifting down to stroke the side of my face. "You are a beauty, you know that?"

"Not so much that anyone's noticed," I said, and to myself, *Not for quite some time.* But I didn't want to be thinking of Roger now. I put my hand over Len's, bringing me back to the present. "Thank you." I kissed the back of his hand. "You'd best be getting us on our way, and pay attention to the road. I don't want my last ride to be in this old thing," I said, teasing him with the memory of the fabric clerk's attention.

The ride home was easy with good traffic, soft afternoon light and the music of our youth, coming from the car's ancient eight-track player. Len had a box of tracks that he'd picked up at flea markets, so Fleetwood Mac, Steely Dan and Mason Williams accompanied our trip in the powder blue Thunderbird. We laughed, hummed and sang together, something we used to do.

When he'd parked at my house, he took the sack from the trunk that had the bottle of sparkling cider. "Chill this please."

Once in the house I was tempted to give in to Len and just throw dinner to the winds while we explored our mutual desires in the bedroom. But my caution button was still flashing. When I put on an apron, he insisted on tying the strings. Seemed there was nothing this boy couldn't make a move out of.

In the kitchen I peeled his hands off me while I was bringing salad fixings and steak from the fridge. "Hey," I said, to keep him busy with something besides me, as interesting as that was. "A fire would be nice tonight. Help take the chill off the house. Could you do that?"

"I don't feel any chill," he whispered as he closed in behind me while I was chopping lettuce for the salad. His voice rose as I pulled away from him to pitch the lettuce into my mrytlewood salad bowl. "But I do wonder if you want to be cutting lettuce with a knife. It needs to be torn, by hand."

"You'll find firewood in the garage. Sam and I put it up while he was here. Go on." I pointed him towards the door. "If you want dinner, get out of my kitchen and attend to warming the house."

"Okay, milady." With his hands raised in surrender, he backed out of the kitchen. "I will warm your house."

"Then we'll eat."

"With dessert to follow?"

"Depends on how you warm the house."

I finished chopping the head lettuce, cut up veggies and threw them together with some variety lettuce that Roger had called frou-frou. I wondered if maybe I should have left it out, it seemed everything had a memory...but life, even about lettuce, must go on. I added kalamata olives, and reached for the blue cheese, but thought better of it. What if Len didn't like blue cheese? Cutting off several generous pieces, I put them in a bowl with a sliced apple.

On the stove I had asparagus ready to steam, and potatoes baking in the oven. After greasing the cast-iron skillet and leaving the steak on the counter beside the pan, I checked to see where Prince Charming was. He can be a bad cat when raw meat is left unguarded. I looked in the garage, where Len was still chopping kindling.

"How's it going there?" I suggested he probably had enough to get a fire going. "I'm just waiting on you getting it started before I put on the steaks."

"Okay." A bit curt. Perhaps he was not used to working for his dinner.

I didn't see the cat. Back upstairs I set the table. Before long Len came up with a box of wood. The dining area was open to the living room so I could see him working on the fire. He soon had a nice blaze going. He followed me into the kitchen, washed his hands. "What can I do to help?"

I put the steaks in the pan to brown and pointed to the salad bowl. "To the table, and light the candles, please." When he returned, I flipped the steaks, and pointed to the tray that held the baked potatoes I'd pulled from the oven and turned up the stove temp. He came back just as I was taking the frying pan from the stove.

"Wow, that's a bit raw even for me."

"Hold your fire, soldier. I'm just part way through here." He was starting to annoy me with his comments. I opened the oven door and set the frying pan with the steaks inside. "Do you want yours rare?"

"Yes, please. You're doing something different?"

"My usual way, maybe new to you."

"Sure, boss." He was smiling, but not with quite the energy he'd had before. Was I about to screw this up? I just couldn't stand a man criticizing me in my own kitchen.

"Please bring back the plates, okay?"

He brought them to me. "You going to heat these up?"

"Sorry, no time." I pulled the pan from the oven, speared his steak and slapped it on his plate, and put mine back in the oven. I handed him the plate and the bottle of sparkling cider, "Take this in and open it please. I'll be right in."

I pulled out my steak, took it to the table, and took off my apron.

I'd set the table so that we could sit side by side. He rose from his chair and pulled out mine, helping me to scoot it in when I sat down, a maneuver that had always made me nervous. With him it was an easy move. He filled our glasses and took his chair.

He leaned over to nibble my ear. "Finally. I thought you'd never sit down. I was thinking I was going to eat solitary, just like I do at home." He put on a cute pout.

I leaned over and kissed it away. I could feel a fire building in myself.

He lifted his glass and said, "To a lovely woman, a wonderful meal, and the mysteries of the evening."

I lifted mine, clicking the crystal, and sipped at the cool cider. Earlier I'd told him that I'd given up alcohol in any form many years ago.

"Even wine?" He'd been amazed.

"Especially wine." I had no intentions of telling him, yet, of my misadventures with spirits. I didn't think he would understand. If he thought wine wasn't alcohol, he didn't know much about the field in which I worked. If he ever asked, I'd be glad to flood him with information, but for now, that wasn't the focus of the renewal of our relationship. Let sleeping dogs lie.

Thinking of dogs reminded me of pets. I wondered where Prince Charming was. He'd been very friendly to Sam last week, but looked to be hiding tonight. From Len?

I didn't put any stock in his response to Len, The Prince was not the best judge of character and could be mercurial in his choices. The trees beyond the house threw shadows across the lawn. If Prince was outside he would be in soon. I didn't like him out after dark, worried that some wild creature might take him.

I put salad in my bowl. "Have you seen my cat?"

"Uhh, would that be a black and white one?"

"Yes, with a tail like a flag, fluffy and waving about."

"It's in the garage. It was watching me chop wood."

"Didn't he come in the house with you?"

"It wanted to, but..."

I turned to stare at him, "Why?" obvious on my face.

"I didn't tell you, didn't think it of it, really. I am allergic to cats. I have medication, but not with me."

"Oh, swell." I felt my ardor for him reduce a notch. A man

who can't be around a cat? How were we going to negotiate that? I thought of my bed where Prince Charming slept on the other pillow. There's always the couch. Not an attractive prospect. Besides, the cat lies there, too.

"Is your steak rare enough?" Might as well enjoy dinner. No doubt The Prince will be crying to come in, pretty quick here.

"Perfect. You've learned to cook. I like this salad, too."

"You want some blue cheese?" I handed him the small bowl of apple and pungent cheese.

"No. That's all right. I like it most times. This just smells pretty strong to me."

"I don't think it's the cheese," I said as I became aware that the fireplace chimney seemed to be making a whooshing sound I'd never heard before. The aroma of the fire had moved from gentle woodsy to the sharper smell of a bigger blaze, with sound. Alarmed, we both went over to the fireplace.

"I think..." Len ran to the front door and out onto the lawn, where he yelled back to me, "Call the fire department! Flames are shooting from the chimney."

I ran with wooden legs to the phone on the side table, not even thinking of the cell in my pocket. Later I would laugh at that. At the moment I was in a barely restrained panic that showed in my voice.

"Here, fire in my chimney!" I shouted at the 911 operator who was calmly asking, "What is the nature of your emergency?"

"Sorry." I took a deep breath and answered her next questions about my name and address. "But it's not so easy to get onto our road."

"Not to worry, ma'am, the fire department knows exactly

where you are and are on their way." I heard then the scream of sirens, a long ways away, but definitely moving in our direction. "Ma'am, you need to leave the house."

"I'm okay. The house isn't on fire."

"Ma'am, your chimney is on fire. Your roof might be engaged. The wall could be on fire. You need to leave the house."

I didn't want to leave the comfort of her voice. Sense had returned to me. "Here's my cell phone number," I said, rapid fire. "Please give me a minute, then call on it, okay? Please?"

"Yes, ma'am, but you will leave the house. Now."

I touched the phone in my pocket, grabbed a jacket from the hallway and met up with Len on the lawn. The phone rang just as I reached him. I answered it, it was the 911 dispatcher. "Yes. I'm here. Thanks for calling back."

"You're welcome, Mrs. Buler. You are outside now? Is anyone else in the house?"

"No." Then I remembered and turned to Len, grabbing his arm. "Prince Charming. He's in the garage." I started back towards the house.

He caught me before I could move. "No! You can't go back in!"

The scream of the sirens was just down the street and then the red truck swung into view and our driveway. Len had parked his car beside mine, in front of the garage. The device to open the garage door was inside my car.

The fire truck, lights still flashing, was huge in my driveway, dominating everything. The driver and rider climbed out of the cab, four firefighters piled off the truck. They were all garbed in tan fire coats with yellow florescent stripes and those snazzy black firefighter helmets. At least two were women.

A fire car pulled up behind the truck, and a man got out. He came towards us across the lawn. His helmet was white with the word CHIEF on the side.

"This your place? Anyone inside?"

Len shook his head: *no.*

I nodded: *yes.* "My cat's in the garage."

Len said, "I think it's a chimney fire, sir."

"But no people inside?"

"But my cat—"

"We'll get to the garage in a bit. Must see to the chimney and building first."

I knew that Prince Charming was probably flying about in the garage, going from window to window to see what was going on. Of all the cats I'd had, he was the most curious, wanting to be in the center of everything, not making a fast run to hide like many.

"I have the door opener right here. I'll open it up right now." I had retrieved it while the fire truck had been pulling into the driveway. I went to push the button.

"Oh, no, ma'am." He took it from my hand and stashed it in one of his many pockets. "We'll want to control the rush of oxygen to the house. My people are on the roof now, and in the house, checking the flow of the fire. They'll camera the wall, go into the crawl space and TIC it." At my mystified look he said, "Oh, sorry, Thermal Image Camera, looking for hot spots." His phone rang, he answered it, listened, said, "Okay. Good. Ready to mist? I'll come help finish it up." To us he said, "Doesn't look to be in the walls, but we have to make sure."

"Look here, Chief," said Len.

The chief looked at him. I could see his eyebrows rise at the demanding and self-important tone of Len's voice. He tilted and lowered his head, saying nothing but the movement encouraged Len to continue. Despite the controlled chaos around us Len had his full attention.

"I just built that fire less than an hour ago. It couldn't have set the house ablaze."

"That's good to know. How long's it been since you had your chimney cleaned?" Stern. Firm.

Len took a step back. "Hey! It's not my house."

"Yours?" His look swung to me and I took a step forward, to him. My guilt made me defensive and aggressive.

Several men pushed past us, holding and pulling a hose, everybody working together, helping get the hose up to the people on the roof. I pulled my attention back to the chief.

"Yes. I've been planning on getting it done. Didn't think it was so immediate."

"I'd say it's right now. Quite immediate. We'll talk about this later. Now I'm going to see what they've found. It was a flue fire. We'll close up the fireplace then mist the chimney. Puts out the fire with a fine spray. You just might have got lucky. This doesn't look to be too serious."

In fact, I was lucky. They hadn't come in with a hose through the front door and blasted everything to a soaking ruin. The job done, the fire fighters allowed us to return to the living room where we met with the chief. "Well, folks, you can get back to your dinner here. Looks to have been a good one. Sorry it got messed up."

"Oh, thank you!" I was so grateful that the whole deal had come out all right. The Chief pulled off his hat and shook hands with both of us. He was certainly less severe than he'd been when he was admonishing us for not getting the chimney cleaned.

"You can find a chimney sweep in the yellow pages. I advise you to call one. They'll come out and fix that for you. Here's my card if you have any more trouble. My cell number is on there if I'm not at the station." He handed me his card, with his name in bold letters, DANIEL DEE. Little wrinkles crinkled at the edge of his golden flecked brown eyes as he smiled at me.

I smiled back and tucked it into my pocket.

To his crew he said, "Men, and women, our work here is done. Let's vamoose and leave these people to their dinner. Good thing it didn't burn, huh?"

With that they all left the house, pulled off the roof, reloaded ladders and hoses back onto the big truck and lumbered out of the driveway, negotiating their way through the gaggle of watchers clogging the entrance to my driveway. The watchers dissipated, eventually.

Len and I went back inside to the dining table. "Perhaps we could take up where we left off?" he suggested.

"I'm not sure where that was." Frankly, my desire for him had cooled. "Why do you always have to set people off? Challenge them?"

He looked at me with wide eyes.

"Oh, don't *wide eyes* me. You know you put that fireman on edge. Just like you did the counter girl this afternoon. Why do you do that?"

"You mad 'cause I was flirting with her a little? Seemed to me you were pretty quick to make sure that guy knows that I don't live here."

That was so opposite what had happened that I stared at

him. I started to clear the dishes off the table. Someone had blown out the candles.

"You know what? I'm just not hungry anymore. I think it's been a long day and perhaps time for you to go home. This conversation is going nowhere. We're both upset by all this. The house smells like smoke. The dinner is cold. I'll pack up your steak and potato and you can take it home and reheat it. Would you like some salad, too?"

"Whatever. I didn't mean to make you mad." He tried to put his arms around me, make nice. I wiggled out of his grasp, went to the cupboard where I keep the container boxes, pulled out a couple, dividing up his meal between the two boxes. He watched in silence as I put them in a paper bag.

"I'm not mad. Just tired, frustrated with myself for not having seen to the chimney. That was something Roger always did, and I just kept putting it off. And I truly am tired. This has been a hellacious week, and tomorrow I have to go back over to Willamina to tend to Magda and Sam. And the quilt."

With one hand he took the bag, with the other he put his hand behind my head and pulled me to him for a kiss.

I let him do it but it was one-sided. I wondered what had happened to the passion. Went up in smoke, I guess.

"I'm going with you, remember?"

Appalling thought. "No. I'll go by myself. It will be simpler. Bound to be chaotic, the less of us the better."

He accepted that. Maybe he wanted the space as much as I did.

"I'll call you tomorrow, on your cell."

I could barely wait for him to leave. I stood outside on the porch until I was sure he was gone, his headlights shining down the driveway in the dusk. When I went back into the kitchen, I heard a scratching noise. *O, Lord, Prince Charming. How had I forgotten him?*

I also realized I had forgotten to take the garage door opener back from the Chief. I opened the door and stepped back as Prince's black and white fuzzy body shot past me with a sharp, "Meow!" His disgruntlement was clear as he passed me, making sure to not brush my legs.

"Sorry, Prince. I've been a bit involved, here." I followed him to his food bowl, which I topped off. I took his water bowl to the kitchen sink, refilled it from the tap. He was mad at me, didn't even look at me while he nibbled and took a short drink. I took my plate to the fridge and put plastic wrap over the whole thing. Dessert had not gone as I'd planned, so I took out the coffee ice cream from the freezer and spooned myself a decent sized bowl. I ate it while I watched a few minutes of late news.

The ice-cream took Prince's attention. He came to sit on the floor at my feet. When I was done, I scraped the bowl so the spoon made that particular noise he was waiting for. I handed the bowl down to him. He licked it clean and walked away, satisfied.

I followed the Prince to our bedroom. He had forgiven me, was lying on the other pillow, waiting for our nightly cuddle. It really had been a long day.

And I was mad at Roger. Never here when I need him. The Prince helped. He was, in the long run, a forgiving creature. Despite all the drama of the day, I slept well.

In the morning I had a message on my cell, a short text from Magda: *Here? Noon? Sooner? Work to do. Problem with wrestlers. Call me.*

Problems with the wrestlers? What next?

I called her. She said Sam thought he had an easy fix. I told her about the fire, she told me we'd work on everything when I arrived, that none of this was an emergency.

Chapter 25

Putting It Together, and Taking It Apart.

I felt remarkably light the next morning. Glad I'd not given in to the lusty feeling that Len always aroused in me. My curiosity about sex with him remains a mystery. I had been hoping to prove my theory that mature sex would be more satisfying than when I was barely twenty. Experience does, in the long run, trump the ingénue.

I ate cold cereal and toast, and coffee. Took a quick shower and dressed in khaki pants and a yellow tee shirt. The chief had told me that I was also lucky because the fire had whooshed up the chimney and quickly burned itself out before filling the house up with smoke. But, still, I would be glad to be away from the faint reminder. Who knew what today would entail? How Tom got dead in the back yard of the quilt cottage? Police activity? And the quilting.

I was rather anticipating the quilting, spurred by yesterday's purchase of fabric. And intrigued, trying not to be dismayed by Magda's statement, "You won't know whether it all works until it is done."

I filled the food and water dishes for Prince Charming, cleaned the litter box and locked the cat door. I didn't like him wandering without me at home, nor did I want another creature using it for entry. When I left I could see him sitting on the sill of the laundry room window, watching me.

When I arrived at Magda's home, her first words when she opened the door were, "You won't believe what that stupid woman has done!"

My mind reeled with the possibilities of which stupid woman she could mean. "Who? What?" I took off my coat and laid it over the back of a dining room chair.

Sam came down the hallway from his room. "I'd guess you are talking about the Quilt Show snafu?"

"How's that?"

Magda said, "The new girlfriend—okay, maybe she's his wife—who took over scheduling the wrestling meets doesn't even know we exist. I guess. Maybe she hates women who sew." She must have seen my eyebrows lowering, because she came to the point. "She's got us sharing the same space, at the same time."

"Oh. Well, just get her to change it."

"Can't. It's printed up on posters already. Gotta give it to those wrestlers, they do promo good."

"So, she gave 'em a date and didn't check the calendar?"

"Yes. Can't blame her. Wasn't on there. It's always been the same, second weekend in November. She's new so didn't know it. She's not a quilter." This last was said with a dismissive shake of her shoulders.

"A real outsider, huh?" I felt protective of this woman I didn't even know.

Magda looked at me with that lowered head.

Sam, standing just behind her, grinned and made a face at me that said, *let it go*. He was right. This little venting of my resistance was getting me nowhere. "Are we going to get some quilting done today? I'm ready to work."

That got her attention. "I'm ready. We have about an hour before I have to go to the police station. Sammy's gonna go with me." She put her hand on his shoulder and sighed deeply. "You don't know how grateful I am that I don't have to do this alone."

I followed her to the sewing room, and Sam said he was going to be outside playing at the roses.

"Can you believe it, Annie, he's going to trim that dang arbor up, make it safe to walk through again. Here." She led me into her quilt room. On the long table were Aunt Sophie's pieces, plus the length we'd bought yesterday.

"You're ready to go with Aunt Sophie's quilt, I see."

"No, Annie. If you're gonna work with this you have to make it yours. You need to decide how you want it to go. You can keep to her plan or come up with your own design. With the pieces mostly already cut out, you do have restrictions on what you're gonna have. Unless you want to take all these pieces and cut them into smaller shapes and re-configure them." She was at them, now. Stroking the nap of the purple velvet appeared to calm her.

I suddenly felt proprietary, walked over and finished the job of laying them out. "Lord, no. I'm just going to get this done, and that's it. I'm not into coming up with my own design."

Magda laughed. "Well, then let's get this done." She sat down at the sewing machine. "You want to do this or you want me to help you?"

"If you do any of the sewing, I'll not be able to say that this is my quilt, will I? For the show?" I swear, until I said that I didn't know I was going to enter the quilt.

"No, you can have help, but, you're right, to make it your

own, you need to do the work yourself. But, I can help."

"I need the pins. And that magnet thing I bought." I pulled up a chair beside her. She led me through the process of threading her machine, and filling bobbins.

"Here." She handed me my packet of yellow flat-headed pins and the other of round heads. "Try it with both kinds of pins. I'm going to go make us some tea and check on Sammy. I'll be just outside if you need me."

I hardly knew she was gone. For the next half-hour I played with the pins, joining the pieces together, following Sophie's paper plan. The pins were sharp and I poked my fingers, laughing to myself as I sucked on the little drops of blood.

Magda came in after a while with a cup of tea that she set down near me. I took a sip then moved it to a side table where I couldn't spill it on the quilt.

"How's it coming?"

"Good. No problems. Other than I remember now that I hate working with velvet. The way it slips around, out from under my fingers, like it has a mind of its own. Good thing I have lots of pins. Have to secure it well before I join the stuff to the 'cord."

"Yeah. Not something I would have chosen." She stood back and looked down at Sophie's pattern. "But then, I wouldn't be making up my own design, either."

I was back at it, holding the fabrics firm as I led the needle through them. "It really will be my quilt. Sophie's and mine."

"You can get part of the front piece done this morning. I've got a couple calls to make, and then Sammy and I are going over to the Hall. Sammy swears we can do both, the wrestling and the quilt show in the same place."

"At the same time?"

"No, silly. But we need to take a tape measure over there, and meet with the manager of the Hall. Then we're going to the police station. You can stay here and work on your quilt. Or if you want to come with us we can pick you up on our way back."

The last place I wanted to go to was the police station. "I'll be good and keep the home fires burning, safely, and work on the quilt. Want me to make lunch?"

"We'll pick something up. You just relax. Only thing I'm going to need when I get home is hot tea. If I get home. If they don't throw me in the hoosegow for not knowing what happened to Tommy." Her face started to twist up like she was gonna cry. I was happy to have Sam appear right then.

He must have seen what was about to happen. "Hey! We've got things to do. No time to worry right now. Save it for later. If they throw you in the clink I'll organize a rescue party and we'll break you out." He patted her shoulder.

She laughed a little through the tears that she reined in with a swallow and a deep breath. "Okay."

They left and I fell into the stitching. My fingers moved along the ribs of corduroy. I was glad that I'd done all that pinning as I held my tongue tight against my top lip to help my fingers keep the velvet and corduroy on track under the steady click-click of the machine needle.

The flathead pins were easier to pull out as I went along, but the round heads were easier to grab. I kept the yellow dish close by my right hand, it was a tiny pleasure dropping the pin to the holder and having the magnet grab it. *Oh, I am easily amused.*

Pleasure was growing within me as the pieces began to

form a shape. Curiosity tickled my mind in a new place it had not been touched before. I seldom thought about Len. The fire chief, however, did come into my mind. As did the events that Magda and Sam were working through. With relief, I returned to the stitching.

Chapter 26

Sam's Report on Scheduling Snafu

God only knows what is going on in the minds of these women, I'm glad to be able to be here to help straighten them out.

We were to meet Lena at the VFW hall, where they show their quilts. The representative of the lodge and the representative of the Wrestling Meet were both to meet us there. Magda knew the lodge guy "from way back," a man by the name of Russ Thompson. The wrestler fella was Big Juan. I kid you not.

Lena is the co-coordinator of the show this year. According to Magda, she'd lobbied hard to get the job. She had presented a list of the quilts she'd entered over the years, and the number of times she had won Best Quilt Over All—three—not to mention the number of times—eight—that she had taken the Blue Ribbon for Best Hand-Quilted Quilt.

Magda parked us by the back door. As we went in we heard shouting. In the middle of the room was our feisty Lena up in the face of a man dressed in skin tight leopard pants. She was yelling, "You can't have your smelly bodies anywhere around our quilts!"

Leopard Pants shouted back, "Then, get your quilts outa

here."

By the time we made it across the room, another man, his arms in the air, looked to be trying to defuse the altercation, had lost his cool and shouted, "Come on, now. No need to be screaming at each other."

Magda stepped around him to take Lena by the arm. She gave a good jerk and Lena had to step back or fall on her butt.

While Magda took Lena aside for a heart-to-heart. I introduced myself to the peacemaker—Russ, he said he was—and said to Leopard Pants, "Big Juan?"

"Sure am. Just call me 'Big.'" His sleeveless t-shirt allowed his muscles to flex, which they did now. Close up to this full glory I restrained an urge to put my hands over my eyes. Instead, I focused on his feet, shod in shiny gold brogues. Where did this man buy his clothes?

We all shook hands as I said, "I'm Sam Smithers, here with Mrs. Buler to help iron out this problem."

"She's the problem to fix," Big said.

Magda kept one restraining hand on Lena's arm. Her other hand went to her mouth to cover her smile as she took in the full splendor of Big.

Lena shook off Magda's hand. Her jaw was set, her posture rigid.

Her gaze flicked to the leopards, and her eyebrows went up. She looked at us, her expression changing to *why are you here?*

"Lena, to get this all straightened out, we must work together. Sammy has an idea. Let's give him a listen, okay?" Magda knew how to work this girl. Lena bounces between being flirty and being angry with every man she meets, looks like to me. With three of us here she chose to be agreeable.

146

Big Juan had to have his say, of course. "This is your problem. We will be having our match as we've advertised. Period." He crossed his arms.

"And that's where we can work it out," I said. "The conflicting match is on Friday night. The Quilt Show is Friday and Saturday, during the days. Right? We just need some help from you and it will work to everyone's satisfaction."

Russ was nodding agreement with me, but Big Juan had his own cranky going.

"How's that?"

"It's simple. On Friday the show will close long before the matches start. Plenty of time for Russ here, with some lodge guys, and you with your wrestlers—plenty of muscle there." I couldn't help myself, but he just nodded." Together, you can get the quilt frames moved to the wall, lickety-split. Heck, Lena, You might even get some customers to come back the next day and buy one of your super-dooper hand-done jobs."

Juan took another look at her.

She colored up. The pink cheeks made her attractive. Maybe this would all work out, get her off my case, and onto his.

Russ stepped up. "Let's step into the office and coordinate time schedules. We'll have to get together early enough to get the space cleared to turn it from Show to Arena, and back again."

We all followed Russ to the office at the side of the hall.

All except Magda. "Great. I'll leave you now. I've got another appointment."

"You're going to stay, right?" said Big to Lena. To Russ he said, "You can show us where we should move the quilts to."

While he was talking Magda walked out, after calling back

147

to me, "I'll be back to pick you up. Or come on over. The station is just a few blocks. Somebody can tell you where."

Wait a minute, I was supposed to go with her to the police station. She seemed awfully eager to be rid of me.

So Russ, Big, and I worked it out with Lena's aid.

"At no time is anyone ever to lay bare hands on a quilt. No matter large or small. I will raid the Guild kitty to buy several cotton gloves of a size large enough for your man hands, to make sure."

"Miss Lena, will you be here to guide us?" Big said.

"Why, of course. Especially if you want me to help you, that is."

"It would be a pleasure, Miss Lena."

"Oh, just call me Lena." She did that dang simper thing. "I'll be here with gloves on."

"Okay, Lena. And after the match perhaps you could show me the highlights of nightlife in Willamina?"

She simpered again, and then laughed, something I seldom saw her do. "That won't take long. Our bars aren't that exciting."

"Oh, Miss, I mean Lena, I won't be wanting to see your bars. You don't think I'd endanger a body like mine with alcohol, do you?"

"Well, Big, honestly, I hadn't really thought much about it. It's something to ponder, for sure. But we don't have juice bars or any fancy stuff like in the city. You mean yogurt, stuff like that?"

"Oh, I think for one night I could let down my guard enough to have pie and a good herbal tea."

Working around their flirting, Russ directed us. We set

the times to make the changes, complete with a list of who was to do what, and when. We all got a copy. I took one for Magda. I left Miss Lena in the pure hands of Big and walked the few blocks to the City Hall where the Sheriff had an office.

A truck rolled past me, carrying a full load of logs with bark on them. Seeing as my son owns and drives a log truck, I was happy to see the business doing well here in Willamina. What says *Northwest* better than a load of logs on the way to the mill? With one part of my mind I saluted the log truck driver, with another I wondered why Magda had gone alone. Was there something she didn't want me to know?

Chapter 27

Magda Reveals The Autopsy Truth

My knees were knocking as I walked into the Sheriff's office. Wish had called earlier, said the autopsy results were in and they'd appreciate me coming down this morning if I could. "If you can't," he'd said, "I could send someone to get you."

That was not going to happen.

Up until I was at the VFW, I'd not known I wanted to be alone when I heard the results. I didn't even want Sammy, though I was glad he'd be here, later on.

Wish and I were old friends. He'd been my Prom date when I was a sophomore and him a senior. It was never a romance, but a close friendship that we've kept for years. I was still proud to be his friend, but this way of relating was new, and uncomfortable.

Tommy had been my husband. A bad one in the long run, but we'd had some excellent times, day and nights, in the early years. Watching Lena and Big Juan spar over the space, I'd realized what a waste of time arguing is, how inconsequential most of my fights with Tommy had been. I wasn't thinking right then of the awful ending of our last time together and the ugly things he'd said to me, and the ugly things I'd said to him.

The counter person was Linda, a gal I'd known for years. "I'm here to talk to Sheriff Kelly."

She played it cool, as if she didn't already know the whole story, greeting me like I was there to collect for a charity drive. "Is he expecting you?"

"Yes." I didn't elaborate with words like "autopsy", or "dead husband in my back yard", or any such thing, though it all flashed through my mind. I also thought about Lena shooting the bear and didn't mention that either. When Linda indicated the waiting bench, I took a seat and looked for a magazine. None. The walls were bereft of artwork, no plants on stands or pots sitting on window sills to ease the starkness. All business and a hard one at that.

I didn't have to wait long before Wish came out and beckoned me to follow him. I feared we would be going directly to see the body but he took me to his office. "I don't have to identify his body?"

"No, he was identified when we found him." He motioned to the chair opposite his desk, sat on the corner of his desk, and sighed. "Here we go." He opened a box beside him and pulled out a clear, plastic bag that had written on it, in black marker pen: *Evidence, Thomas Buler.* It also had the date. But I didn't see that at first. What I saw was a piece of cloth that I recognized immediately. Little machine-embroidered, blue and purple spring flowers all over against a pale yellow background.

"Oh, my God!" popped out of my mouth.

"You know what this is?" Wish laid the bag down on the desk.

I reached for it but he put his hand out.

"You can't touch it. It's evidence. Can you tell me what it

is?"

I'd recovered my startled wits. "Can you tell me where you got that?"

He flipped the box closed, set the bag and cloth on top and moved to the chair behind his desk, like we were having just any old conversation.

I expected him to ask if I wanted a cup of coffee, like they do on television cop shows when they're trying to put the suspect at ease. To distract them. Instead he said, "How about you answer my question first, and then I'll answer yours?"

I stalled. "That's part of a piece I bought years ago. Why do you say it's evidence? Where did you come upon it?"

"Not yet. What did you do with the material? Was it part of one of your quilts?"

"Fabric, please, not material. Well, sure, I used some bits of it in a crazy quilt of leftover pieces I made some years back." I was getting exasperated with this man, my *friend*, "Where did you find this piece?"

"How about you tell me? My wife sews and she is particular about her cloth. She knows where every piece is, and what she used it for. Stop playing with me. I know you don't let go of your 'fabric' easily, especially if you like it a lot. I gather most of it's not in the crazy quilt. Where did this piece come from?"

"You're asking me to tell you where *you* found a piece of fabric?" I was scared now, as I did know what had been done with that fabric, but I didn't want to tell him until I'd talked it over with Sammy first. My face must have showed that I knew the answer to his question, but I answered it with a small distraction, a white lie, if you will. "I gave some to a friend. I've not seen it for a long time, now, so I don't know what happened to it."

He wasn't distracted, but I could tell he was becoming annoyed. "The cloth? Or, the friend?"

Details, he was going for the details. "The cloth. I don't know. Doesn't matter. I used up the pieces I had left. Not sure I remember when I saw it last. Please tell me where you found it."

"Fair enough. It was gripped in your dead husband's fist. What was his dominant hand?"

"Huh?"

Wish stood up. "Please, Magda, stop stalling. I think you know what happened to that fabric. You need to tell me. Now."

"Right. He was right handed." I was having trouble breathing.

He handed me a bottle of water.

I unscrewed it, took a deep breath, and then a shallow drink. I could barely swallow, my throat was so tight.

I whispered, "She made a dress with it."

He stared at me for what seemed a long time, and then said, "This dress, did it have a pocket?"

Another small drink. "Yes." I screwed the cap back on.

"Where?"

"The left side."

"Then if he'd been falling, and grasping as he went down, he could have pulled the pocket off with his right hand, if he was facing the woman?"

"I suppose so." I unscrewed the lid again, took another drink.

"Now, will you tell me who was wearing that dress?"

"I don't know who was wearing it!"

He glared at me.

I'd given the fabric to Lena and she had made a shirtwaist dress from it. One with a breast pocket. This looked the right shape for that pocket. Yellow threads hanging from where it had been torn loose. How?

My mind jumped around for a different answer, but none came. I told him the truth. "Okay, Lena made the dress. She was very pretty in it, too. She's rather old-fashioned looking, you know. With the way she does her hair, the dress was right. She liked to wear it when she wanted to look extra nice, like to parties. But I don't know if she was wearing it when the pocket got torn off.

"Surely, you don't think Lena had anything to do with Tommy's death?" Once started I couldn't stop. "She and Tommy never got on, you know. Her snippy mouth and his controlling ways. He always said she never knew her place with a man. I always figured he thought that 'cause she wouldn't give way to him in anything. Even when he knew best, like about fishing.

"She'd belittle the catch he'd bring in, saying if he'd just exerted himself a little more, gone out farther, not given in so early, he could have brought in bigger ones from deeper down. He'd say something then like maybe he wanted to get home to me, but that since she couldn't keep a man she wouldn't know anything about that." I ran out of steam then, and looked at him.

"How could this all tie in with Tommy being dead?" I sounded pitiful, so I inhaled, breathing confidence into my words. "I'm sure Lena doesn't have anything to do with this."

"Lena would be the one to answer that. We will be asking her."

At that moment a woman said, through the speaker on Wish's desk, "Hey, Sheriff, a guy named Sam Smithers wants to come in. Says he's with Mrs. Buler."

Wish looked at me.

"Oh, yes. I'd like him here." To myself, I said, *now*.

Sammy came in and I introduced him. They shook hands.

To Sammy I said, "Wish—I mean Sheriff Kelly—and I went through school together. He knows I couldn't have done this."

I plopped back in my chair while Wish pulled up a chair for Sammy. He moved it so he was sitting close beside me, his shoulder touching mine.

Wish gave the touch a glance but I didn't care. In my short time with Sammy I felt closer to him, and safer with him, than I ever had with Tommy. And I didn't care who knew it.

Tommy had been, at the end, a worthless husband. I knew that I'd done my best to be a decent wife, but then, I'm not perfect. My widow weeds aren't going to be spotless, either. I put my hand on Sam's knee.

Wish said, "I'd like to agree that you couldn't, but I don't know any such thing. I think it's time to talk more to Lena. Do you know how I can find her?"

"Wait," said Sammy. "The autopsy? What did this man die of? Shot? Strangled? What? I thought that's what we were here for?"

Wish started towards the door, motioning that we were done. "Yes, we know what killed him. You'll know soon enough. We'll get Lena and meet you in an hour at your studio."

On the way to our car he said to Sammy, "You be there with Mrs. Buler."

Chapter 28

Back at the Studio

When Magda and Sam came back to her house I was ready to stop sewing. Soon after I started putting the pieces together I'd discovered a mistake in Sophie's work. Her diagram didn't jibe with one of the sewed pieces. I could see where she'd started to undo it. Some of the threads had been cut, but then she'd abandoned the project.

I knew she'd hated fixing. I could remember her voice when she'd tried teaching me how to sew, frustration adding an edge to her words. "Annie, this piece here is not right. You have to rip it out."

I'd glared and grabbed the piece with both hands to rip it apart.

She had stopped my hands with hers. "No, here." She handed me a little thing that looked like a cuticle pusher but with a tiny sharp knife on its end. "This here is a seam ripper. You'll be using it more than you're gonna like, but it will be a good friend in the end." She'd held up my mis-sewed piece, slipped the little knife in, began undoing my precious work.

Made me mad. I'd reached to take it from her hands, managed to get in the way and got a nipped finger.

"Don't get your blood on it," she'd said. Then, "I hate ripping out my work. But sometimes, you just have to do it."

I had a clue as to why she'd abandoned this project.

It had waited several years but finally, I'd corrected her job, feeling just the tiny bit superior at my patience, and yes, at my re-sewing of her seam. The piece now fit correctly into her pattern.

I'd been going gangbusters on the thing and feeling confident, until I ran out of cut pieces. I needed more fabric. From Magda's stash in the closet of her sewing room I found a mauve and cream checkered fabric that I knew would liven it up and bring the zing it had been missing. I wanted to use my untried tools to measure and cut. For that I needed Magda.

And tea and a sweet. They came in and found me at the fridge, taking out a jar of strawberry jam to set beside the jar of chunky peanut butter.

One look at Magda's face and I knew I was done sewing for the time. Her hair was shaggy like she'd been running her hands through it, again.

"You must come with us. I have to get a quilt. Wish wants me to bring it to the studio. He's bringing Lena."

"To your studio? Why?" She'd gone down the hall, so I looked at Sam while I found the bread and a butter knife.

"They found a piece of fabric in her husband's hand. I'm not sure what he's thinking, but looks like it might be something that both Maggie and Lena have to do with."

"In his hand?" A vision came up that wasn't pretty. I nearly put away the idea of the sandwich, but with me, hunger for something sweet always overrides whatever's going on. I took a bite and then a drink of milk. That helped quell the queasy that had started with the vision.

157

By the time Magda returned with a quilt in a good sized tote, I'd finished my lunch and cleaned up. Magda said she'd rather I drove, so we went in my car, with her and Sam sitting close together in the back seat. I wanted to ask questions but had to focus on making the correct turns up into the hills to the place she'd once described to me as her place of serenity.

I wondered how she felt about it now, the place where her husband had been murdered and buried? I hoped today's quest would put the questions to rest, but perhaps I should fear the answers even more. Magda was so close to Sam's heart.

What does that quirky Lena have to do with all of this?

I parked beside The Sheriff's car in front of the cabin. Only the sound of nervous breathing from the backseat was witness that I wasn't alone.

Sam said, "Don't worry, it's gonna be all right."

Magda didn't answer, but opened the car door, stepped out and reached back in for the quilt. She stood there a moment, gripping the handles of the bag and looking at the straggly bushes by the front door. "Gotta neaten that up."

Sam came to stand beside her. "I'm your man." He linked his right hand in her left. I came up behind them and heard him whisper, "Okay, girl, let's get this over and done with." We went around the side of the house to the back yard.

Sheriff Kelly and a deputy stood under the apple tree near the empty grave. The hole in the ground still gaped. The tree looked forlorn, with a few apples hanging. The ones on the ground were drawing yellow jackets. Their humming was the only sound.

Off to one side were Deputy Bybee and Lena. Sheriff Kelly nodded as we went to stand next to Lena.

"Our need, now, is to find out what happened, and why," he said. "I have reason to believe, Lena, that you have the answers."

Lena made as if to leave.

Deputy Bybee held her in place.

Lena sagged in defeat, but not in submission. She shot straight up again, wrenching from the deputy's grasp. She grabbed Magda's hand and pulled her to the edge of the ragged hole.

"None of them will understand, but you. You have to. It was awful! He's...was...a terrible man. He scared me!"

Magda pulled her hand free.

Lena screamed, "Don't leave me alone, Mag. Please. I didn't mean to ruin your life!"

Magda reached for Lena's shaking hands, wrapped her own around them.

The sheriff stepped close to them. "Ms. Veil, I have something I want you to see."

She recoiled and shrieked when the sheriff put his hand into his jacket pocket and pulled out the plastic bag with the piece of fabric in it.

"That don't mean nothing. That's just cloth."

"Magda, I believe you have something in that bag. Can I see it?" When she handed him the bag, he put it on the picnic table and pulled out the quilt. "Grab the other end here, let's open it up," he said to the other deputy.

Lena's body hunched. She opened, then shut her mouth.

The sheriff pointed to a piece in the crazy quilt design, a pale yellow, flowered piece. "Do you recognize this fabric, Ms. Veil?"

She leaned close to look, twisting her mouth. "Uh, yeah. We all made stuff out of it."

He laid the plastic bag on the quilt, beside the fabric she'd admitted she knew. Though its contents were brown and dirty, there was enough design left to see that they were the same.

"I understand, Ms. Veil, that you obtained some of this cloth from Mrs. Buler. Correct?"

She glared at Magda, shrugged, and then nodded. *Yes.*

"And that you made a dress from it? A dress with a breast pocket?"

Lena leaned to look close at both pieces. "Yes."

"This other cloth matches, does it not?" Before she could answer he said, "Is it from the same piece?"

Lena was sniffling, "It could be. But it's a mess. Where did you get it?"

"From Tom Buler's hand. His dead hand. He took it to his grave with him. I guess you didn't notice when you buried him." Her face went blank, until he leaned back against the table, against the quilt.

"Don't lean on the quilt!" Lena snapped.

If it hadn't been out of place I'd have laughed.

"That piece of fabric was from your dress, wasn't it? Will you tell us how it got into a dead man's hand? Now! Stop fooling around."

That was all it took for her to crumple, literally. Her knees bent and she wobbled.

Magda caught her on one side and Sam hauled her upright on the other. Deputy Bybee took over, moving the quilt to one side and helping Lena sit on the picnic bench.

Lena's mouth was crimped tight against her teeth, and

her hands were on her face. Finally she took one big breath and started talking.

Chapter 29

The Truth, Confession

"It's not like you think. Magda, I never meant this to happen. I'm still not sure what did happen." Lena reached out and latched onto the nearest end of the quilt, pulling it to her lap. Part of it fell to the ground. She didn't notice. Her hand worried the piece she'd clutched, like a child worries a blankie. She directed her words to Magda, as if they were having a heart-to-heart, but with all of us watching, and listening.

"You remember, Magda, when you went with the gals on the last Quilt Shop Run, in June, and I didn't go 'cause I was working to finish that commissioned piece from the woman in The Dalles?"

The sheriff straightened his back like he was going to tell her again to get on with it, but Deputy Bybee lifted her hand ever so slightly, and he relaxed.

Magda said, "Yes, I was gone longer than usual as we were making a long sweep to take in a couple shops over in Boise. Gone four or five days."

"Barely long enough," Lena muttered. Louder she said, "That first night I went to a pie social at the church and wore my yellow dress, the one I made from the fabric you gave me. The new pastor is single. With nothing to do afterwards I came here to finish the quilt. I was in the living room watching one of the BBC shows I'd taped, steeping myself in the accents. I felt good about being almost done with the quilt. Just sitting there, turning down the binding, drinking my tea... I like being alone here sometimes.

"I heard a noise at the back door. Scared the crud outa me, coming so sudden. A key turning in the lock. I yelled, 'Who's there?' and then wished I'd kept quiet."

She gave Magda a quick glance. "We keep an extra key in a fake rock by the door. Who'd know it was there but you and me? You know how the key sticks in the lock just that little bit, and then the door makes that scraping noise when it does open?"

Magda nodded.

"It did that and then I heard someone step on the kitchen floor. Somebody yelled, 'Damn, Magda! Ain't ya got this door fixed yet?' and I relaxed. It was Tom! Never thought I'd be happy to see him. You know, he and I never got on, but at least it wasn't some crazed killer looking to chop me up and spread me around the woods."

Lena stopped talking. Deputy Bybee handed her a water bottle and she screwed off the lid and took a big gulp. "Thanks."

She handed it back and gripped her blankie again. "I put the quilt to the side and went in to the kitchen. What a sight! He was drunk. Ugly.

"Oh, he seemed happy enough to see me 'Lena! You old thing! What'cha doing here? Where's Magda?'

"While I was answering his questions I started making coffee because he needed to sober up. When I asked him how he got here and what he was doing here, he got rude. 'I live here, you stupid woman!'

163

"Except he didn't call me 'woman', he called me the c-word. I'm not going to repeat it. He was foul.

"'You don't live here! This is our studio. You live on your boat.'

"Then I realized what his being here meant. 'Where have you been? Magda's been trying to get in touch with you for a long time. We figured you were dead.'

"'None of your damn business. Maybe I've found a good woman who knows what a man needs.'

"I guess I sneered at him then because he swung at me, throwing himself off balance. I stepped out of the way and he stumbled against the counter. 'Where's Magda?' he said.

"When I get scared I do get defensive. I guess I did that then. 'As if you care.'

"He shouted, 'Listen, bitch, tell me where my wife is!' and doubled up his fist.

"I was close by the magnetic knife rack by the sink. Without thinking I grabbed the fillet knife.

"He reached around the island to take it. I slashed out and cut the fat part of his thumb. He leaped back, roaring filth at me. I pulled open that door and, funny, it didn't stick.

"I ran outside. He was right behind me. I have never been so terrified in my life. I just ran, blind, into the back yard. He grabbed my shoulder, spinning me around. I slashed again, not aiming. He dodged back, but on the downstroke the knife cut into the top of his leg.

"He screamed and snatched at my head, had my hair in his hand. His hands were everywhere. He snagged my pocket I guess.

"He fell and grabbed his thigh, screaming, 'Bitch! You cut me! You've hurt me!'

"I couldn't see much in the dark. The leg of his jeans did have a big slice in it, and it looked wet.

"I ran back into the house and watched him through the window in the door. I was so scared. He was crying and screaming, and then he just went quiet and fell over.

"When he hadn't moved for a while I went back out, scared he'd jump up and grab me. But he was still. So still. His eyes were open, staring at me. Accusing. I think I lost my mind for a while 'cause if I'd thought it through, as I've done a thousand times since, I'd have called for help. I never meant to kill him. Didn't even mean to hurt him, but he scared me."

Lena stared at Magda. "He scared me!"

"Yes." Magda didn't move from where she was standing, but she leaned forward to touch Lena on her shoulder. "Yes. I know. When he was drunk he was very scary. And dangerous."

Lena turned to look at the sheriff. "All I could think of was hiding what happened, wiping it out. Cleaning up. Making it disappear, like it never happened.

"I went to the garden shed, found the shovel. I picked a place as close as I could get to him and dug in. The ground was soft because we'd had a lot of rain. I kept going until I had a hole deep enough and long enough to put him in. It wasn't as much as I wanted it but I just had to get him covered, to get those eyes away from my sight.

"It took a while to get him rolled in. I had to push and pull at his legs and then his body. He didn't move easily. No help from him. When I got him in I saw the knife on the ground, and threw it in the grave. I didn't like seeing him and that knife just laying there on the dirt. In the garage I'd seen a raggy quilt so I got that and threw it over the mess. Then I shoveled all that dirt back over him.

"It was dark but I could see that the grave was obvious, so I moved the picnic table over it. Hard to do on the soft ground. Pushing and pulling, lifting it to sit over Tom's grave. Do you remember, Magda, when you noticed the table was moved and you remarked on it and I said I'd done that because I'd been doing my e-mail on my laptop and the sun was in my eyes, so I moved the table. And you never questioned me." She leaned forward to Magda, her arms out in a plea.

Magda moved over beside her. Lena fell into her arms, letting loose, finally, with an anguished howl.

Sheriff Kelly watched, saying nothing.

I stood by Sam, wanting to leave, to go in and sit at the kitchen table. I'd watched the whole drama with a feeling of detachment. A criminal client had told me that sometime people, "Confess to impress." The phrase kept repeating in my mind as I listened to her. I wanted to believe her and I could see that Magda did believe her, or at least understood how Lena could have killed Tom.

I could believe that Tom caused his own death by his threatening behavior, that she killed him in self-defense. Still, it was ugly.

The sheriff motioned for Lena to stand up.

Magda stood with her.

"Lena Veil, You are under arrest for the murder of Thomas Buler. You have the right to remain silent..." He continued with the Miranda statement while Lena and Magda stood together, holding hands. When he'd finished, he said, "We'll take Ms. Veil to jail now, where she can call a lawyer. Magda, you must let go of her."

"But Wish, this is unfair. Can't I take her home with me, and bring her in tomorrow? She won't run away. She'll be with us." She included Sam in this plan.

Sam shook his head at her naïveté, while Sheriff Kelly rolled his eyes.

"I would if I could, Magda, but you know we can't do that. There's a way these things have to go and she's got to go through with it. You can best help by getting in touch with her people. She is going to need help. She'll probably be out tomorrow on bail."

Sam held out his handkerchief to Lena. She wiped tears from her face, and when she was done, I was amazed to see her face smooth, calm, and smiling, peaceful. A wobbly smile, but a smile.

When she went to hand the cloth back, he said, "Keep it. You might need it again."

Lena, the sheriff, and his officers left.

Sam, Magda, and I went in to the kitchen and sat down at the table, but in a minute she was up to put the kettle on. She reached into the cupboard for cups, and then looked at the empty spot on the knife holder beside the sink. "Funny, I never noticed the knife was gone."

"We'll get a new one," said Sam.

"The sheriff didn't mention it either." I said.

Magda sat down, took a sip of her tea. "Ow, hot."

Considering that the murdered man was her husband, she seemed quite calm. I was reminded of the peaceful expression on Lena's face. She explained to us, and to herself, "They already have it in evidence. They had an idea of what happened before Lena spilled it all. They did an autopsy so they knew how he died. Just needed the details."

I try not to be a counselor to my friends, but she needed to talk, and here we were. I took a drink of my tea, put the mug down. "So, Magda, how are you feeling now?"

"What do you mean, how am I feeling? Am I supposed to be feeling any certain way?"

"Well, then, let's start with what you think about how Lena feels. Did you notice how peaceful she was after she'd dumped all that?"

Sam said, "Yeah, that was odd. She's been an absolute pill the whole time I've known her, and suddenly, she's peace and light. After she'd just confessed to killing a man."

I gave him a look to let Magda talk.

He nodded and sat back in his chair, taking up his cup.

At that Magda put her hand out to him and laid it on his. She then told him the full horror of her marriage, his drinking, his craziness. "Lena knew more about his behavior than others because she was here and had seen him. But it had been so long, I'd begun to hope he would never return. Funny, I remember Lena saying, when I talked to her about it, that maybe I was lucky, maybe he was gone for good.

"I told her I'd like to know that for sure. Have some paperwork, some proof." She took a deep breath. "But I've got to help her. Tomorrow, we'll go get her out of the lockup and make sure she has a decent lawyer." She eyeballed me as she rinsed her cup and left it in the sink. "And then you and I, we have a quilt to finish!"

Sam was looking at her in a funny way, almost flirty. "Mayhaps you will need to finish up some things with your husband, too, Maggie. Then you and I can get to our business."

"And what would that be?" She took our cups, put them beside hers in the sink.

"Simple. Getting to know each other. It's about time, and I don't have a lot of it, or at least not as much as I usta."

"Okay, you guys," I said, as we locked up the studio and got into my car. "I have to get back home to my cat, get a sitter for him, take care of a couple of things. You two have plenty to do tomorrow, and that doesn't include working on that dang quilt. I'll be back day after tomorrow. You can expect me before noon. Anything I need to know before then, you have my number."

I let them out at Magda's house, Sam helping her out of the car and she opening the front door to let him into the house. It pleased me to see them helping each other. I felt a tiny shiver of envy, but shook it off. So be it.

The drive home was lonely. The stark truth of how Tom had died was painful to think about. But I could see the justice in it.

It was a sober ride, full of reflection as to how some alcoholics luck out, and some don't. I was a lucky one. Someday, when the time is right, I'll have a talk with Magda about this. But not now.

Now is her time for healing. Sam will help.

Chapter 30

By the River

I woke with the dawn, a feeling of purpose and expectation, like on Christmas morning, energizing me. Through the open window above my bed I listened to the chattiness of the Clackamas River. It has a very distinct voice that depends on the depth of the water, high and strident in winter, tumbling rocks, or the slow drawl of summer, moving smooth and low to the Willamette.

Now it was the change of seasons, leaves swirling in small eddies, with the occasional splash of a salmon making its way upstream to spawn. The river melody soothed me to lie like a salmon resting in the shoals of the edge of the river. The day could wait.

The change of seasons, Fall to Autumn, Spring to Summer brings chemical changes that are felt by us, an energizing need to move towards the coming change. In Spring we build, dig and plant, reveling in the smell of opening up to the outdoors to nest. Now, with the nip of autumn I welcome another blanket on my bed, gather and store the harvest, stack wood against the winter. Sam had helped with the winter wood, so I was good there.

Purpose and expectation. Eventually these two feelings

took me from my bed. I stretched and thought of doing a few minutes of yoga before coffee, but Prince Charming was twining around my legs and I gave over to him. I swept him into my arms where he tried to nuzzle underneath my chin, which made me giggle. I was on the move so he squiggled to get down, hitting the wooden floor with a thump. I followed him to his feeding place, found the water low and bits of dry cat food scattered around the dish. I replenished the dishes while he pranced around, mewing.

He happily tucked into his breakfast while I attended to my coffee and Sam's Cheerios, with a side of raisin toast with cream cheese. I sat at the kitchen window, looking over the lawn to the trees and the river. While I munched I listened to my phone messages. Four of them.

Len: "Annie, are you there? I'd hate to think you are listening to this while in the arms of the fire chief. Oh, I forgot, you weren't flirting with him. Just kidding. If you find time in your busy schedule call me. I know you have my number."

Fire Chief: "Mrs. Straw, I'm chagrinned to admit that I have your garage door opener. Forgot to hand it back to you the other evening after your flue fire. Please call and tell me when it is convenient for me to drop it by, or you can pick it up at the station." He left his cell number.

"Chagrinned?" Sounded like a voice from an old English novel. Intriguing, a man of language.

Len again: "Annie, I have news. Call me."

The fourth was from the Gladstone library. A book on tape was overdue. I'd finished it on the way home last night, so I'd take it in today. Go to the fire station while I'm in town? Or call the cell number? Hmm, a small flutter?

I was going to have to call Len, but decided I needed to walk down to the picnic table before I did anything else.

I refilled my coffee cup, with Prince Charming following every move I made. We had walked only a few steps out of doors before I felt the chill. "Go chase a leaf or something. I'll be right back." I fetched my beloved sweater, the wool one with sheep on the pockets. Warmer, I walked the brick path to the table above the river. Prince rushed across the lawn to scare a couple robins into the trees.

The crispness of the air sent a tiny shiver through me. Prince played with a leaf picked up by the light wind. There were more leaves on the lawn than just a couple days ago. I sat on the bench and leaned back against the table, watching the river.

I recalled the last time Roger and I had sat here, him tired and weak, me aching with his pain, unable to do much beyond be there. I switched off the melancholy that threatened to overwhelm me, because it felt more like something I *should* feel than what I was really feeling. I wanted to live in today, not the past.

Vitalized, I made the first call of the day. It was early but I wanted to reach Len before he went out.

He answered, his voice thick with sleep, "Whoa, Annie. Do you realize it's only a little after seven o'clock? A.M.?"

"It's daylight. I thought you'd be catching shots of the sunrise."

"Funny." He made a quick recovery. "Want breakfast? My place? I have eggs and bacon, can do something fancy if you want."

"Oh, gosh, Len, thanks, but no thanks. I've already eaten. Out here on the river it's late, nearly midmorning. The birds have already forgotten first light. I'm just getting back to you, and wondering what news you have. I have some for you, too. You'll never believe what went down last night."

"I'm in the show. Officially."

"What show?"

"Don't be stupid. The Willamina Quilt Show, of course. With *Tumbling Blocks*. The one that won a blue at the State Fair."

"Well, for Pete's sake, Len. That's cool. You'll probably be competing with me, but I don't expect to be any real competition, for now. Besides, mine is a combo quilt, designed and partially executed by Aunt Sophie, but re-designed and finished by me. So how do you like them apples?"

"I don't think I'm going to worry about you as a competitor, not a quilting competitor at least."

"Len, you say the nicest things. Thank you for reminding me of why we're not together anymore." What a jerk. And me such a fool for being attracted to his sexy ways and cute looks. No wonder he wasn't married any more, if he was as push me-pull you with her as with me. I found interesting that bit he said about us being in competition. Therein was the problem.

I didn't want to compete with my mate, I wanted to walk side by side with him, with us helping each other as needed, not always looking to see who was ahead. His cute butt had made me forget why we'd ended the first time. But I had encouraged him, had to admit it. Now, how to bring us to a place of friends, not at odds or angry with each other. I didn't want anger, but could welcome an old friend.

He wasn't done. "I have something else in the show too. A surprise. Those people like me, so I'm giving them more than *Tumbling Blocks*."

Right now was not the time for The Discussion of Lover to Friend.

"Len, let me tell you about yesterday. Lena confessed to

killing Magda's husband, and burying him in the backyard of their studio."

"I must say, I'm not surprised that her sharp tongue killed someone. Tell me."

I did. That took me until the sun had moved from behind the hills to shining highlights on the ripples in the shallows. I signed off with him, saying I needed to do some housekeeping before I went back to Willamina tomorrow. I declined his offer to accompany me. Back in the house I put in a load of wash, gave the house a lick and a promise, refilled the cat's dishes and left extra water and food in case I was gone a couple of days.

With chores done, I called the fire chief. It was nine-thirty by then. I figured any self-respecting fireman would be up.

He was.

I launched into who I was, but he stopped me.

"You're the woman with the flue fire. Certainly I remember you. I still have your garage door opener. I'm embarrassed, but I wanted to be sure your house didn't shoot to a full blaze."

"No, thanks to you. It's all good."

"Did you find your cat? Is he well? He had an unusual name, 'Charmer'?"

"Close. Prince Charming. Yes, he's fine. But I need my opener. I've got another one, but I don't know where it is"

"I'll bring it by today if you will be home."

"Give me a time and I'll be here. No commitments today other than to keep the cat company, maybe rake the lawn."

"Eleven?"

"Agreed. Or, I could come in and get it from the station."

"No need, I don't go into work until one. That'll give me

174

plenty of time."

He was right on time. I was expecting the fire hat and coat, but he was dressed in a brown sweater over a blue-flowered Hawaiian shirt, with brown slacks. Light hiker boots. No hat. A nice mix of casual and ready-to-work. In his right hand he had a white sack.

He answered my greeting with, "I've got your door opener." He handed it to me. "And I brought a little something to go with coffee, if you have time." A sparkle of humor in his warm, golden brown eyes.

I bit back a response of having all the time he needed and invited him in. The door opener was warm from his pocket, and I enjoyed the feel of it in my hand, a gentle intimacy.

In the kitchen I busied myself making a fresh pot of coffee while he looked around.

"Cheerful room. It feels wonderfully open with these windows. Mind if I sit down?"

"Please do." I opened the sack. Large cinnamon rolls, two of them. "Maple frosting. I love these but never buy them, too much of an indulgence. How sweet of you."

"Not as sweet as they'll be. I figured I have to make it up to you, after stealing your opener. I've never walked off with private property before." He handed me another one of his cards. Daniel Dee. "Call me Dan."

"I'm Annie. Welcome to my kitchen."

I poured our coffee and dressed our plates with the rolls. I cut into the sweet roll and took a bite. "Gosh, this is good, where did you get it?"

He named the local bakery, run by his cousin, "But she doesn't give me a discount. Not anymore. I buy too many of them."

I wondered if he has other women he takes them to, and felt a twinge of jealousy. *Silly, this man isn't in any way mine. His honest face can't belong a Romeo. Please not.*

I'd noticed a faint resemblance to a mature Harrison Ford who I will forever see swinging across the void clutching a terrified Princess Leia. Dan's eyes sparkled with humor and wrinkles appeared when laughed. Good hair, originally auburn? The red highlights were now graying. Looking at him, I felt emboldened to follow my intuition that nothing happens by accident.

"Would you like to come to dinner tonight? You fed me." I cut another bite of the roll, "I'll feed you." I could barely believe I'd said it. Suddenly struck, I said, "You're not married are you?"

He laughed. "No. I was once but that's been some years ended. She wanted greener pastures than a fireman could give her, I guess. No girlfriend, either. Are you suggesting a dinner date?"

Now I was shy. "Just saying. I haven't been in town very much lately and like to know my local firemen. Never can tell when such a contact could be handy!"

He laughed as I put the light spin on my forwardness. "I get it now! You think if you feed me dinner I'll clean your chimney. Everybody's looking for a discount!" He got the coffee pot, refilled both our cups.

Whew, I thought I'd scared him off.

"I'd love to eat dinner with you, but not tonight. I'm working the long shift tonight. Tomorrow?"

"I won't be here tomorrow. I'm working on a project in Willamina, a quilt project with my cousin and some friends." That was certainly skimming the cream from the truth. "I'll be

176

there for the next couple of days. And then I must check in with The Prince."

He looked at me over his cup. "The Prince?"

"My cat. The one that was locked in the garage during the chimney fire. I have a neighbor who usually looks in for me but she's out of town right now, so I'll need to come back in a couple of days."

"Tell you what." He took his cup, plate and utensils to the sink, gave them a quick rinse and set them on the counter. "You're busy, I'm not so much so right now. Let me make sure I've got your cell number in my phone, and we'll be in touch over the next couple of days. Okay? Now, I've got to go to work."

We did the number business, and I walked him to the door. "What are you doing for the rest of today, while I'm slaving over a hot fire engine?"

"Prince and I have leaves to rake, laundry to finish, and for me, a trip to the library. Early to bed tonight for an early morning tomorrow."

He said, "I'll go past the library on my way to work if you want me to drop off something. "

I gave him the CD's and watched him drive away in his Ford pickup. Not flashy like a fire truck, but still a good, serviceable vehicle. I might miss the T-Bird, but not much.

Chapter 31

The Cleansing

Prince was watching all my moves when I left the next morning, before first light. I'd stocked him up on everything, except company. Maybe another cat? Have to give some thought to it. I hugged him goodbye. He wiggled away and ran to the laundry room where he could sit on the dryer by the window and watch me leave. I doubt he saw the little wave I gave him as I backed out of the driveway.

It was a good drive. Mists in the hills, coming into Willamina, past the Timbertown sign. The pale gray sky illuminated the tops of the hills in black and white. As I drove through the town, the soft russet and oranges of maple trees and sumacs glowed in front yards.

Magda's place was looking spiffy. Sam had clearly been at it. The Cecil Brunner rose arbor was especially tidy and easy to walk through without snagging at my hair or clothes. The maroon leaves of her Japanese maple had crisp points and it looked as if it had been fluffed. A Tropicana rose by the door was blooming its last summer glory of orange and yellow.

I let myself into the house with the key she had given me. The house had a different, indefinable, feel to it. I followed soft voices to the enclosed sun porch at the back. Magda and Sam were sitting together on the wooden swing suspended from the rafters, her head leaned lightly against his. They were watching the sunrise color the sky a spectacular pink and yellow and soft blue, and shared a coziness, a comfort that hadn't been here before. Together.

They didn't hear me until I stepped onto the brick floor behind them. My smile matched theirs as they looked at me. Sam put a foot down, stopped the slow movement of the swing. "Hey, pretty girl! Come on in. Join the party. We're just watching the sun rise. Coffee in the kitchen if you want some." The table in front of them held cups and toast. They were in their jammies and robes, hers a soft yellow terrycloth, his a cotton, old fashioned, blue check.

I thought Cary Grant. I fetched coffee and sat down in an easy chair to the side of theirs.

"Here," said Magda, "pull that over so we can see your face." I did and they told me about how yesterday had gone. They had procured a lawyer for Lena. The judge determined her to not be a flight risk, so she was able to bail herself out.

"She feels guilty about killing Tom, even in self-defense. I told her I understand and forgive her. My only problem is that she didn't tell me sooner. I wouldn't have spent all these months looking over my shoulder afraid I'd look back and there he'd be."

Sam gave her hand a squeeze. "Well, that's all in the past now. We'll take care of Miss Lena, and you girls get that quilt show done."

Again, the hints. What kind of plans, I wondered. It didn't feel to be my place to be asking that, right now.

Magda put down her coffee cup. "I've got a call to make today to my friend, Mila. She's a spiritual healer, I need her to come cleanse that grave. I want my place of peace and sanity back. But first, I'm going to shower and get dressed. Nature Boy here has a few more tasks to do in my yard, and while he's at that, you can be working on the quilt."

I told them about Len being in the show. Magda was okay with it. "It's good to have a man quilter. We like the diversity." She laughed. "I saw his *Tumbling Blocks* entry at the Fair. It deserved that blue ribbon." She turned back. "By the way, how're you two doing?"

Put on the spot I shrugged. "He's rather heavy-handed. The truth? I'm looking more towards the fire chief."

They said together, "What fire chief?"

I'd told them about the flue fire, but none of the details about Len, or the fire chief. Now I told them about the impromptu brunch and the sometime dinner plan.

"Sounds," said Sam, "like you are ready to come out of that box you've been in. And I'm glad to hear it. You know I'm not a fan of Len. But whatever, whoever you choose, be easy on yourself. I went through that you know, it takes a while to be steady again." He looked at Magda, "That means you too. 'Cept, I think you've been alone long enough! I'm curious about that cleansing of the ground."

I too was curious, but Magda wanted her shower and she promised to explain later.

I went into the quilt room. There was the quilt, ready, just as I'd left it. My eagerness to get at it, to be adding the checked piece and perhaps something else, surprised me. I could hardly wait until Magda could help me with the next step.

We'd stashed the rulers and mat in the cupboard. I took them to the table. Time to use the fancy gadgets. The rotary cutter and pins were where I'd left them by the front piece. I was petting the velvet when Magda came in. "Looks like you're moving along well. It's time to cut the check and add it. But first, a little figuring."

"Oh, no, not the math." Working the lengths and widths in her mind to know what size pieces to buy, and to cut, is easy for Magda. "I don't know how you do it."

"There is no trick to it, Annie! I will teach you. Don't worry about it. You have the talent."

I raised my eyebrows.

"No, you do. I know you didn't think you could change Sophie's quilt, but you've already spiced it up."

She was right about the rotary cutter, it was a slick tool, but I was cautious with the sharp edge as we cut the check. She helped me pin the check to the block. "Oh, I do like it!

"I wonder what else you'll do with it. It's worthy of entry at our show. You'll be proud." She stood up and waved me to the machine. "Sam and I must go fetch Mila. She is going to cleanse the place where Lena buried Tommy. Even though he's no longer there I can't be at the studio without thinking about it. We're going to pick up Lena for the ceremony, and I've asked Wish as well. We figure to be at the studio around four. You will come, too, please?"

"Of course. Is there anything I can do?"

"Yes, there is. I need tobacco, a packet of the loose kind. And we must feed Mila. You can pick up the tobacco and a pre-cooked chicken, perhaps some chips, and some salad makings. Bring a jug of fresh, local-made cider, too. Here." She handed me a twenty-dollar bill. "While you're shopping you can be planning, figure out what is going to be your back piece. I'm in favor of the check for the back."

She turned to leave, but then turned back. "If you could be at the studio before four and air the place out, I would much appreciate it."

I worked on Sophie's quilt until near two o'clock, and left it flat so I would see it first when I returned.

I felt somewhat goosy as I entered the studio kitchen and looked through the windows into the backyard. Someone had filled in the hole and raked it smooth, but the dirt over what had been the grave was mounded and darker, still quite visible. I didn't know what Magda and Mila had planned, but was glad that something more would be done.

The studio felt dark, whether because I knew what had happened there, or whether my sense of the place changed when Thomas was unearthed I didn't know, but the mound gave me the heebie-jeebies. I didn't like being there alone. I busied myself with putting away the groceries, bringing down plates from the cupboard, setting out utensils on the counter. I was relieved to hear a car in the front driveway, and voices as people came inside.

Wish Kelly wore plain clothes, Magda had on a sky blue skirt and a white blouse with a yellow, flowered vest. Lena was dressed in black slacks and a thin tan sweater over which she wore a hip length black jacket. Her expression was tense.

The woman with them must be Mila, a small woman with a serene expression on her deep brown face. Behind her came Sam, like the sheriff wearing jeans and plaid shirt—the equivalent, for many Oregon men, of dressed up.

Sam set the basket he held on the picnic table.

I handed the pouch of tobacco to Magda.

She did the introductions.

Mila's black hair was gathered at the back of her neck in a long braid. Over a long-sleeved black tee she wore a red vest printed with native symbols, spirals of eternity, shafted

182

arrows, mountains shaped of triangles. Her long, dark blue skirt brushed the tops of sturdy black oxfords. Around her neck was a beaded necklace, with a small leather bag hanging from it. She wrapped her hand around it occasionally as she talked.

I gave Lena a hug, and felt some of the tenseness leave her body as I released her. She was near tears. She went to stand by Magda, who took her hand.

Mila led us to stand around the mound, close to each other, and began to speak. "The feather of an eagle is sacred." From the basket on the table, she took a dark feather about a foot long with a shaft half again that length. The shaft was beaded in a diamond design, with several thin strips of white leather hanging from it. "The spirit of our winged friend will help in our purification ceremony."

She held the feather by the beaded handle, gently moving it from side to side. "Magda has told me the ugly thing that happened here. The spirit energy from a tragedy can hang around unless we help it along, to go on to its own healing. We are here to help the spirit of Thomas. We're also here for the spirit of the bear.

"We call on the four directions: To the East." She raised the feather. "To the South." Turning full circle, she offered it to the West, and then the North. After returning the feather to the basket Mila took out a large shell holding a herb bundle of silvered, dried sage that was several inches long, a candle, and matches.

"The smoke of sage will cleanse." She lit the candle and set it back into the bowl. Her cheekbones came into high relief and a glow lit her dark eyes as she held the end of the sage bundle in the candle flame. It took some perseverance but it finally caught. She shook it to extinguish the flame, leaving an aromatic smoke to rise.

"The smoke will carry away the negative spirits that remain here, or that we bring with us. If you have a problem with the ceremony you can say 'no' as I come to you, and I'll pass you by."

If Magda had asked for this to be done, I was in.

"First, we will smudge with the smoke, then each of us will have a chance to talk to the spirit of the man who died, or to say whatever you want. Magda, I will start with you."

She moved the smoke up and down in front of Magda. With her hands Magda pulled the smoke onto her head. Breathing deep of the aromatic tendrils, she washed her face in it. She turned around and Mila bathed her back in the smoke. Magda turned around and said, "Thank you," to Mila who acknowledged the respect with what sounded like, "Ah ho!" She repeated the smudging for Lena, Sam, Wish Kelly, and me. She handed Sam the bundle. "As our elder would you please smudge me?"

"With pleasure." Sam followed Mila's lead as if he was familiar, and comfortable with the action. When he finished, Mila took the bundle and returned it to the bowl. She set the bowl, still trailing smoke, on the mound. The small flame of the candle flickered.

She stood still, her head tilted towards the sky, murmuring in a low voice. The late afternoon sun cast color onto the high clouds, outlining them with silver. A robin settled down on the grass some feet from us, cocked his head, hopped a few inches, tilted his head again, and pecked sharply at the ground. As Mila continued to pray, the robin snagged a worm and flew away with it.

Mila's voice became louder. I heard again, "Ah ho!"

Peace settled into me.

"I have asked forgiveness from the spirit of the bear for the taking of his life without respect." She opened the tobacco packet, took out pieces and sprinkled them onto the ground. "Lena, you might also want to do this, to let the spirit of the bear go."

Mila turned to Magda. "You asked for this healing. Creator and His spirits are with us. Now is your time to speak."

Magda took a deep breath. "I want to speak to Tommy. I don't know if your spirit is here... I hope so. I've been so angry at you. I've hated you. I'm glad you can't hurt me anymore. That's awful to say but it is what's in my heart. I want to change that now, to release you, and myself, from this pain we've put on each other. I did love you." Her voice faltered and her tears flowed in a stream. Silently she brushed the tears away with her left hand, her right still tight within Lena's grasp. "That's all I have to say now."

Mila looked at Lena and nodded.

Lena released Magda's hand and clutched hers together, as if she was praying.

"Oh, God. I feel so awful. I killed this man." She took a deep breath and continued. "Tom, you know I didn't mean to. I wonder if you can hear me, can feel my sadness. My sorrow. I don't know if I would make it different if I had a chance to do it again. I was so frightened of you. I pray that your spirit can leave now. I want to let you go. I want us both to be free. I forgive you. And I forgive me."

She let her hands fall to her sides, bent her head. "Amen." When she raised her head, there was a gentle smile on her lips. No tears. "Oh, yes," she took the packet that Mila offered. "Bear, I'm sorry. You were just being a bear. And I was a scared woman. Please forgive me." She sprinkled tobacco onto the

185

ground.

Sam spoke then. "Man, if your spirit is listening, I say to you, you can go on your way now. I'm here to help Magda, with or without your blessing. But I hope you go now to a restful peace. This place needs it. So does Magda." There was an edge to his voice. "I'm done." He nodded to Mila.

Mila said, "Mr. Sam, think about this. Are you done? This ceremony is a cleansing of all our spirits, including yours."

"You want more from me? I don't even know this person."

"But you have anger at him, anger that is here, now. I'm asking you to find a way to give that negative energy to the smoke. This is the time to let him go on his spirit journey."

Sam seemed to consider her words. Asking Mila's permission with a look, he took up the sage. Bringing it closer to his face, he blew on the pale red embers, rekindling the smoke. "So, Tom. I don't suppose you meant this to happen. I've made a mistake or two in my life too." He stopped, and then said, "If your spirit is really here I sure don't want to be the one to keep it here. So, I let my hard feelings for you all go up in smoke." He held the bundle in front of him, took a deep breath and blew into the smoke.

He handed the bundle to Mila. "Hey, give me that tobacco, please." He tore off a large chunk, that he shredded into smaller pieces. He sprinkled them over the mound. "Dang! I feel better. Hope that all worked for him."

"Thank you, Sam." To the sheriff and me she said, "Which of you wants to go first?"

We didn't have much to say. He muttered, "Rest in peace, man."

I said, "Amen," hoping I didn't sound flip.

Mila brought the sage bundle back to Magda. "Anything

else?"

"I'd like to smudge Tommy's spirit."

Mila waved the sage, bringing forth a good blaze on the end of the bundle until the smoke was heavy. She handed it to Magda. "Release him."

Magda looked in front of her as if she could see him, waved the smoke in a long, deep oval. "Tommy. I pray that you find a place to fish and..." She smiled. "...to ride your board through the tunnel of a long wave. So long."

Mila took the bundle, said, "Ah ho!" and waved it over what now felt to be an empty mound. In a wide arc, she released the smoke to the Four Directions. "We send this smoke into every corner of this yard, through the trees, the flowers, freeing all the creatures from what happened here: the flying ones, the creeping ones, the two legged and the four legged. Let the people who live and come here feel peace. Ah ho!"

Her lips relaxed into a soft smile. She placed the smoking sage into the shell, set the shell onto the center of the cleansed earth, took up the feather. Waving it sharply over the candle flame, she extinguished it. "I think there is food, now?"

We followed Magda into the kitchen where we feasted. For the first time in many days everyone appeared to be happy. Released. I couldn't fathom the why of it, not sure I believed in the effect of the ceremony. But it didn't matter. The peace in the air was palpable and the smell of the sage on our clothes and in our hair filled the kitchen.

Mila said, "I'll leave the bowl and sage here with you. If you like you can smudge the house, inside and out. Anytime. Or not, as you want. I thank you for asking me to do the ceremony."

After the meal Magda and Sam took Mila home. The sheriff

left. I took Lena home.

At her house she gathered her purse, and then turned to look at me. Her face was smooth, without the lines of anger and fear. "I don't know what that was all about," she said, "but thank you for being there. No matter what happens, I feel strong enough to get through it." She hugged me. It was dusk and the outside light came on as she stepped onto the driveway. I watched her go in, and then drove to Magda's.

We would sew and shop tomorrow at the nearest fabric store. I had a couple more ideas to put into action, and was amazed to find that I was eager to talk it over with Magda, to get this quilt done. With the ceremony I found that I'd freed up my hold on Roger, had let him go as well. I didn't understand the how of it, but that night, after a late cup of chamomile tea with Magda and Sampson, I slept like a baby. Free.

Chapter 32

Sweethearts

In the morning I slept late. I was leaving the bathroom a little after eight when I saw Sam coming from Magda's room. He was wearing the checked robe, his hair was tousled, and when he saw me he laughed.

"Caught like a rat in a trap!" His eyes were happy, his back straight.

"Well, well," was all I could say. "I'm going to make coffee. Will you two be wanting some?" I swallowed a giggle which made my voice squeak.

"No. Yes. You make it. I'll come get some for me and Magda. We'll meet you in the sun room." He slipped past me into the hall bathroom. Always a gentleman, he'd left the master bathroom to her.

I went on into the kitchen, feeling more lighthearted than I had in...in maybe years. Between the ceremony last night and this confirmation of my suspicions, the world seemed to be full of light.

I had my coffee and English muffin in the sun room when the sweethearts came in, each carrying a coffee cup, her with a bowl of green grapes, him with a plate holding two toasted muffins. They settled the china on the coffee table and took their places in the swing.

Magda said, "We're going to go shopping, Sam. Get you your own robe." She snorted softly, and her eyes sparkled. "That'll do it for today, but I'm making some big changes around here, starting with cleaning out this house."

I'd not really known Magda very long, but still, this giddy happiness made her so attractive that I would have sworn she was taller, more slender. Her skin had a rosy glow.

"Out with the old." She tugged on the arm of the robe. "And in with the new!"

He leaned over and kissed her.

I wondered if I should be somewhere else. But it was all right. "Good, you can leave me at the nearest fabric shop while you shop for the right robe. For Mr. Cool, here, right?"

They both grinned at me.

"Okay. Just you and me. We've got some stores in McMinnville where I can get everything we need. Sammy, any special color you want your robe to be?"

"Heck, no. Anything you pick out will be perfect. I do like a ribbed robe. What is that called, kinda like a blanket?"

"Chenille."

"Hard to find. We'll see."

I stood up. "I'm going to get ready. Before we go shopping, Magda and I need to consult about Sophie's quilt."

"Is it still Mom's quilt, or isn't it more yours, now?" Sam said.

"More like mine."

Sam said, "I've got to look at it. Sounds like it is going to be special. Zingy."

His statement gave me an idea, but I kept it to myself.

"Oh, gosh!" Magda said. "Time has slipped away from me. This afternoon is Quilt Squares! Gotta be there. You must come with me, Annie." She started to get up, and then relaxed back down beside Sam. "You get ready. I'm going to sit for a minute more with Sammy."

Magda wasn't able to leave me at the quilt store, and run; we looked at fabric together. She didn't much care for the striped pattern I picked. "You have a different color sense than I do, that's for sure. I have faith that you're seeing something I'm not."

Our next stop was at a specialty shop for men's clothes, where she found a light brown robe, of wonderfully deep, soft terry. Accented with clear, red piping around the collar, cuffs and the below-the-waist front pocket, the robe was, as Magda declared, "Smashing! Sammy will look adorable in it."

Two events occurred that afternoon. Len called on my cell phone while I was enjoying the late September sun on an outside bench while Magda finished up her shopping. I watched a black and yellow bee working a mum in a container, no doubt enjoying the sun as much as I.

I wondered if the bee sensed the end of summer, taking with it the bounty of nectar. Maybe it lived in the moment as I was doing. The ring of the cell in my pocket was an irritation, but when I saw it was Len I was curious enough to answer. "Hi. What's up?"

"Where are you?" His tone was demanding. "I've been by your house and your cat's alone."

Huh? I'd already put him in my past, didn't appreciate realizing that just a couple weeks ago I'd of been flattered that he missed me. I wouldn't have heard that propriety tone in the same way. I'd of thought it was cute. Now it annoyed me.

"At Magda's." I'd almost said, Sam and Magda's but he was no longer in my circle of people who needed-to-know anything about me or mine. In a new way, Magda was "mine", too. "We had some things to take care of yesterday so I stayed over. Plus..." This I did feel like sharing with him. "I'm close to having Aunt Sophie's quilt done."

"How could you? You don't know what you're doing." He tried to offend me with the truth.

I laughed. "I didn't, but Magda's been teaching me. Guess what? I'm liking it, and seem to have some talent at it."

"You? Well, it must be in your blood." I knew when his tone changed from, 'Ha, you?' to eager interest that he wanted something from me. "Can I come over and see it? You know, I might have something to offer. You do remember the blue ribbon on *Tumbling Blocks*, don't you?"

How could it hurt? "Sure. Okay, but not until I'm back home. I'll be bringing it back to work on. Lunch tomorrow maybe? You could pick up sandwiches from a deli in town? We can talk quilting, but don't expect to stay long, I've got a lot to do on it to be ready to enter it into the show. You're lucky, already being accepted. By the way, where was your signature? You did sign it, right?"

"You didn't see the signature? It's down at the bottom right, but small. *L. Bolder. 2010.* We can talk about that, where you put your name and date. Whatever." He was completely "old friends" now. "I'll bring the sandwiches. Maybe we can even eat outside, by the river."

"That'll depend on the weather. See ya tomorrow. We can talk rulers and mats and arithmetic."

I clicked off the phone, not sure I'd been wise to ask him to lunch. But what the hey, maybe he could help me understand the math. I hadn't mentioned to Len that Sam would be there with me. Sam wanted to visit his friend in the retirement home again.

Having Len and Sam in the same house could be troublesome, but I'd have Sam as a shield.

Chapter 33

A Quilting Bee

The robe fit Sam perfectly. I swear it made him look younger. Or maybe that was an effect of their romance on both of them? "I'll just leave it here." He smiled his roguish grin.

The meeting of the Quilt Squares was in the room above Sunshine's thrift store on Main Street. Magda led me to stairs attached to the side of the building.

At the top we entered a room that reminded me of an empty hay loft in a big old barn. Windows from all sides plus a skylight lit up the room with natural illumination. Pole lamps at either end of the frame highlighted the work space.

Six women were gathered around a quilt frame. "This is the whole of the guild, except Lena, who's at home today." The first three I'd met with Magda at the Fair. Marge was wearing a quilted vest. Sunshine lifted a mug, asked me if I wanted a cup of coffee.

I shook my head.

Judy smiled a hello as she checked threaded needles on the quilt. Mariah looked to be a twin of Marge. Karleene sent me a reserved smile, and Gretchen, patted my shoulder. "Any questions, just ask."

Magda said "We're working the door prize for the show. A queen. Made of our favorite kind of stars."

Magda directed me to sit at the quilt frame and showed me how to use the thin, threaded needle in front of me to take small stitches. "Just do your best. Four to an inch, or so. A quiltzilla like Lena will do 10 to 15. Perfectly."

"Quiltzilla?"

"A person," said Sunshine, "who is obsessed with quilting."

"Perfect quilting. Unlike us," amended Karleene.

It was a comfortable afternoon, despite the fact that they talked a special language, casually mentioning 'paper piecing', and 'stitch-in-the-ditch'. I decide these women are, despite their protestations of being perfectionists, quilt culters. I feel myself falling into their finely woven net of waxed quilt thread. I was through displaying my ignorance, would look it all up on the Internet, later.

I never thought I'd have so much fun, sewing. These women kept me in stitches. Seemingly oblivious to Magda and Lena's situation, they satisfied some of my curiosity about the quilting history of their town by telling me a true story that involved what the media of 1915 called a Murder Quilt. A woman was accused of murdering her husband but the local women, her friends, didn't believe it. To support the cost of her defense they collectively made a quilt, with scenes from the incident, working on their squares in the courtroom, and raffled it off.

"How'd it all come out?"

"The jury didn't agree with the wife's friends. The story's in a local book, and the quilt is in the archives of the Oregon State Historical Society, in Portland," said Mariah. They went back to stitching.

They went on to gossip about one of the gals who wasn't there. One bit in particular caught my attention. "Didja hear," put in Gretchen, "that Katie Heap is getting a new car?" In an aside to me she said, "Katie is a local gal who sits in with us at the frame now and then. You'll meet her at the show." She continued to the group, "She left that old husband, got a new car, a sporty thing that only seats two. A convertible. Don't think she'll have it long, she's always buying stuff at garage sales and selling it at her booth here at Sunshine's place."

"Yeah," said Marge. "That car is a piece of fancy work, like her T-bird."

"What color is it?" Mariah said.

"Baby blue. Pretty much the same as her 'Bird."

Couldn't be. There are lots of old T-Birds around, lots of them blue.

"That car wouldn't be practical in this part of the country. Could rust up quick in the rain," said Sunshine.

"Don't think that's a problem. She's got a place she stashes it, with a quilter friend from Portland." Gretchen paused to grin, before adding, "Something somebody said made me think the friend might be at our show. You won't miss seeing that car if it shows up, though I doubt if the top will be down in November."

My thoughts were spinning. *Maybe Len knows this Katie person. After all, he did win a blue ribbon and these quilters appear to know each other. I'll have to ask him tomorrow.*

In a quiet moment Gretchen said to Magda, "I am so very sorry about what happened to your husband. What a thing!" She pointed her needle at Magda. "I'm glad that you and Lena are all right. But, it's been so long that your husband's been gone that I'd nearly forgot you were married."

"Well, I am...was," replied Magda, setting aside her needle for the moment. "Yes, it was ugly. Frankly, much of the marriage was, too."

The others at the table kept their needles busy, but everyone was listening.

"It all seems like a bad dream."

"Ugly, but sometimes that's the way it is. I'm ready to move on."

There was a collective sigh. They all were glad someone had brought up Tom's death. The women each added their condolences. We turned again to our needles. Magda sat thinking and then said, with a little snort of laughter, "Oh, I hope our story never ends up in a book." The women looked at each other, someone started to giggle, and soon they were all hooting, including Magda.

I sat quietly, concentrating on my stitching and listening as they explained "paper-piecing".

Marge said, "You put your fabric right sides together then pin the paper on top, the paper with the diagram of what you're sewing. You sew on the lines then fold it back and trim away the excess paper, leaving a small seam allowance. It's a perfect image."

I thought *impossible*, as they rolled the quilt on the frame to expose more top, and went back to quilting. Mariah started talking about a new technique called, "Paperless piecing."

That set me off. I said, "This is all just impossible, and isn't paperless piecing where we came in?" They wanted to demonstrate the techniques to me, but I demurred, "One thing at a time, ladies. You've got me at a quilt frame, more than I ever thought I'd do. I'm going to finish my aunt's quilt, and be done with it. I won't be needing any of that extra info."

A couple rolled their eyes, and someone said, "That's what I thought, too."

I ignored their responses.

Chapter 34

Magda, on Sammy & Love

I'm amazed at myself. I'd thought that older people were past passion.

Wrong.

'Course I've been carrying a torch for Sammy since I met him in Cannon Beach twenty years ago, when I looked into his blue eyes, heard him laugh, watched him paint a cabin door. But I'd kept my feelings to a low flame. I was married. So was he. Potential trouble.

I don't care what the neighbors, or anyone else, think about me being with Sammy so soon after Tommy's death. He's been gone from me for years. Sammy is here to stay.

His skin feels like silk to my fingers. My hands slide over his back with the sensitivity one has when touching luxury, registering every tiny bump or scar, as it rises under my hand. Silk with the slubs left in. The edges of his muscles are more ropy than if I'd grasped them when we were younger, but firm enough to make me feel safe. He can take care of me, but with our ages, we share the care.

I've missed laughing at a man's silliness. When I was in grade school I punched a boy for calling me a silly goose. The other night I put dinner of beans and wieners on the table, saying, "Sorry for the plainness."

He touched my wrist. "You silly goose!"

I laughed. I'm tickled now when the jokes come from my old man.

Sam's hands, what works of wonder. He can do anything with them, cut and tie up roses, whip up scrambled eggs, or, yes, arouse in me sensations I'd thought long dead.

I'm still alive. So is Sammy. The twinkle in his eye that spoke to me those many years ago is still sparking.

Chapter 35

Sam, on Magda & Love

This woman turns me on. Whether she's making dinner, or absorbed in her quilting and doesn't even know I'm there, or lying beside me in bed, her eyes looking deep in mine while our hands explore... She gets this old blood 'a pumping.

We fit together as smooth as butter on a hot cob of corn. And to think, she made the move on me. That second night I spent at her house, I was passing her bedroom.

"Aren't you cold in there all alone?" she called.

True, the nights have been cooling, but I can't say I was chilly. But I heard what she was saying, so I answered, "Why, yes, I did notice a certain chilliness to the room."

"Well, then, I think you might find that this room is warmer."

I wasn't behind the door when the brains were passed out. She was right about her room being warmer. Downright cozy in fact.

I haven't wanted... intimacy... Well, dang it, sex, since Sue's death, not to say I've not thought of it. Until Magda, I have shied away from being, or having a lover. I've had enough to do just taking care of myself and Dave and Teri. Danged if they haven't gone past where they need me. As for the grandkids, I probably reach out to them more than they do to me.

I'm ready to stretch some more, grow again, and that is sure what I've got in this relationship. I'd like to marry her, make an honest woman of her. Don't see that in the cards, right yet. But I'd like some marker that we are special to each other; I want others to know I'm her protector, and her lover. That she's mine, and I'm hers.

I'm thinking on it.

Chapter 36

The Old and the New

I arrived home late from Magda's and stayed up even later, turning Roger's den into my sewing room. I'd brought our quilt with me. The quilt and my fabric fit nicely on the shelves he'd built to display his ship models, with room to spare. I found the table he'd assembled the models on equally suitable for my sewing machine.

Next morning, I rose early. From the car I retrieved my luggage and other quilt supplies I'd gathered while with Magda. Sam had not come home with me after all. Dave had driven over with Teri to pick up a used log truck from a seller in Willamina. At Magda's we stood around admiring it while Sam gathered his suitcase and then, in front of everybody, he kissed Magda goodbye.

Not on the cheek, no. He grasped her about her shoulders and placed a good buss right on her mouth. Dave, who had been about to get in the cab, stopped and watched. "Hmmmmm." He swung on up without another word.

The sweethearts moved to the passenger side and with only the slightest assist from Magda's hand on his butt and his grip on the inside bar, Sam swung into the cab. I imagine those two had an interesting talk on the way home.

Thus my plan to use Sam as a shield had been hijacked, but I enjoyed being alone as I turned the room to its new purpose. The den was an inside room, windowless, but light from the living room windows came through an open arch. Remembering the quilting loft at Sunshine's store, I considered adding a skylight for the light. But for now, the overhead electric lights served well.

I was so absorbed in cutting the stripe for the quilt edging that I was startled when the doorbell rang. I opened the door, Len stood there with a lunch sack in hand. It was from an upscale fast food place in Portland, and no, I'd not yet made coffee. Hadn't even eaten breakfast so the food was welcome. Len, not so much.

When he leaned in to kiss me hello, I pulled back.

"What?" He looked stung, "Am I too late, too early, not the right kind of sandwiches? What?"

"Oh, Len, come on in." I offered my cheek, embarrassed to be treating him like this when we'd been so intense the last time we'd been together. It wasn't his fault I'd changed my mind, not directly. "I'll put the coffee on. I've been so absorbed in the quilt that I've not even looked at the weather. Is it warm enough to eat outside? I had to close the window last night because of a chilly breeze. But looks like the sun has dried the dew off the grass. We can eat our lunch at the picnic table."

I could hardly believe I'd forgotten to make coffee. What was happening? By then I was in the kitchen, where I pulled out my large serving tray, set coffee mugs and napkins on it.

Len was very attentive, setting the sandwiches on the tray, pointing out that he'd brought JoJo's, "Do you have ranch dressing?"

While I put some in a dish he asked if I had any pickles. I gave him a jar and another dish on which he arranged the small dills. When the coffee was done I poured it and he carried the tray out to the table.

Prince Charming followed us out, jumped on the bench by me, and sat there watching us eat.

Fall wasn't just in the air anymore. In a few days the calendar would note its official arrival. September was winding down. We'd had a couple nights of rain, so were lucky to have this sunny day. Recent rains had raised the river's level, and the water moved briskly with purpose to run on to the Willamette, flow into the Columbia, and roll on to the Pacific.

I munched down my pastrami on rye, crunched the pickles, dipped the jojo's and drank my coffee with gusto. Len remarked, "Good thing I got here when I did, you'd have fallen flat onto the sewing machine, starved."

I laughed, "Finally, my knight in shining armor." Whoops, I was flirting with him. Mixed messages. He gets close, I get confused. This is not the direction I want to go. Want to turn him off, not on. "Not really. I'm holding up all right. Just got caught up in the sewing. Forgot to eat. Nothing unusual about that."

He ignored my sudden brusqueness, said, "For you it is." He put down his sandwich. "That's one thing I remember well, you enjoy your food." He turned to look at me, his eyes doing a slow front scan. He scooted closer, put his arm on my shoulder, his hand rested on my neck, his fingers slid from playing with the ends of my hair to stroking the hollow in my throat, drifting downward, while he murmured, "No damage. You look good enough to eat." I'd sat still, yes, enjoying the sensation as he'd leaned closer. But...too close.

I moved back.

His hand fell away as he leaned back to look at me. "What's the matter with you?"

Might as well be now. "I've been thinking, about us. And the past. It didn't work then and it's just not going to work now. We need to stop here and stay friends. Any further and we're going to end up right where we did before."

"How was that?" His tone was chilly. He moved down the bench as if to look at me better.

"You were—are—too possessive, and you're still bugged because I've got interests beyond you."

"Such as?"

"You're gonna laugh. It was my photography, now it's quilting."

"That's great! We can share, work together."

"No. Quilting is a private thing, personal. You know that about it, I'm sure."

"At times, yes. But wait, what's this got to do with us? You've turned cold to me, like you did before. Is it another guy?"

He must have seen it in my face. "For God's sake! It is! Bet it's that damn, know-it-all fireman." Again he saw the truth of it. "Oh, for Pete's sake!"

I wanted to say, *What is it, for God's sake, or Pete's? And who's Pete?* but he didn't look like he could take a joke.

"Well, that just beats everything."

"Frankly, it's none of your business, but it's not the fireman. It's that you and I don't belong together. Something is off about us, always has been. Too much tension. We always end up fighting. Please, before we ruin a friendship, I want us to change direction." While we'd been talking I'd loaded up the tray with the remains of our lunch, now I started to the house with it, "Getting too cold out here for me."

He didn't offer to take it from me. "I'll say. So, maybe you're right." He opened the door when we came to it. "I can back off. I know how to do that. But, hey, I've got go into Portland for a meeting with my publisher, working on another book. Did you even read the one I gave you yet? Probably not, too busy with 'other things'".

I didn't like the sarcasm. "And here I was thinking we were going to talk about quilting math."

"Yeah. Sounds exciting." He did one of his snide smiles. "But it'll have to be another time." He looked around. "Don't think I've left anything. I'll see you at the show, for sure. Oh, I was going to tell you what else I'm going to have in the show, but you'll just have to wait and see. Let me know if you need anything, quilt-wise, now that we've established that's what we are, quilting buds."

I walked him to the door, hoping, I guess, for a goodbye kiss, though for God's sake, I don't know why. He jerked the door open. "Call me if you need help with your quilt."

"Sure. Thanks for the lunch." If he heard me he didn't answer.

Boy, was I glad to see him get in the T-Bird and drive away. Although my delayed dinner date with Dan was hours away, at five o'clock, I didn't want them to bump into each other. My thoughts bounced from Dan back to Len. I wondered about what I'd said to him, about us being not right. My body registered regret that I'd sent him away, but my mind was at ease. I'd got rid of something icky, a chameleon that wouldn't stop crawling over me. Pretty, but I suspected he wasn't showing his true colors.

Chapter 37

Dan

Once I was back to my sewing room I forgot about Len, forgot even, for quite a while, about Dan. I was just working to get the quilt to look like I wanted it to. When I had to re-do some of the sewing to make it just right, I laughed at myself. Perhaps I do have a real bug about the perfection part of quilting. A quiltzilla? I don't think so, but I remembered the Quilter's Standard re: Mistakes: "If you stand back five feet from it and can't see it, then leave it."

I didn't follow that rule. If it bugged me, I fixed it. I had just got the top all together, just needing the binding, when the doorbell rang again. Seemed to me like that's all it was doing today. On the way to the door I saw the clock, big hand on five, little hand on twelve. Dan. Right on the minute.

As I opened the door to him I said, "Sorry, I'm not ready yet," but my mind registered wet comb marks in his hair, like when a kid's hair is especially neat for a special occasion. Awww. "Come on in."

He handed me a handpicked bouquet of yellow mums, and I laughed with recognition. "These look to be from my front yard."

"Huh," he said, "not only beautiful but perceptive."

"I have the perfect vase," I took them from him and, easy as anything, tilted my mouth to his. Our kiss was a lovely beginning to an excellent evening.

I thought we made a fetching couple, he in his brown slacks and striped shirt with a red tie, me in a straight black skirt and just-a-little-cleavage-showing red blouse. Matching without planning. We went to an Italian restaurant in Portland, where we both had spaghetti. During dinner I explained about my original reluctance to quilting and my new fascination with it. He listened attentively as I told of meeting Magda, the whole debacle at the quilt cabin, and the cleansing. "Did you ever wonder if Magda did it?"

"No. I never doubted that she really didn't know why he was so late in coming home. And when it all came out she was honestly horrified."

"It does seem that she might have called the authorities to report him missing."

"Honestly, I think that the longer he was gone the happier she was."

"Boy, that's a rotten way for a marriage to end up, don't you think?"

I agreed, gave him a short history of my marriage. "We didn't have any of that ugliness. But that's the past. I want to know about you. Did you grow up here? Where is your family?"

"Hmm. You know I'm divorced and am living with my mother. You'll have to meet her. I think you two will get along. You both like cats."

"That's a good start."

"Yes, I grew up in the house Mom still lives in, by the river. Dad worked construction. He died about four years ago. He was a good man." His brown eyes darkened and he took a bite

209

of spaghetti while I commiserated about the death of his father.

"Spent my boyhood with my sister swimming in the Clackamas, graduated from our local high school. Marines. Desert Storm. When I got back from that I went to Oregon State, started in journalism, finished up with a degree in geology. Pretty much a home boy. Always wanted to be a fireman like lots of kids do, but I got lucky and am living my dream. Except for being alone. Don't like that so much. I'm a pretty simple guy when you get right down to it."

A soldier. College educated. Solid childhood. Rocks and fire. Reads. I questioned his "simplicity" but kept it to myself. Not time yet for deep probing.

When we came back home I showed him Sophie's quilt and we had a good mug of chamomile tea. He didn't push our mutual attraction. We'd also talked at dinner about not wanting to go too fast at this, about how much we were enjoying getting to know each other. Our parting embrace was lingering and warming. He pulled away from the growing intensity of our kiss before the heat became too intense. "I'll call you, tomorrow." His fingers squeezed mine before he left.

I don't remember my dreams that night, but I know I was smiling when I woke up, feeling relaxed and soft, unlike the stiffness in my shoulders when I thought of Len. Dang! I'd forgotten to ask Len about knowing that Katie Heap woman. Probably didn't matter.

I had coffee and a bagel with cream cheese, and spent the day finishing the top. I took my time pinning on the edging, a loud solid red, then looking at it for another long time. I took it into the dining room to my big table where I spread it out flat and just stared at it some more. I liked the red edge. It gave the quilt a bold finish. I finally gave in and sewed it on. Didn't take long, took longer to take out all the pins. Too many, but like my life, I wanted nothing to shift, not without my permission.

When I was done I called Magda and told her. She walked me through putting together the sandwich of top, cotton batting middle, and back. The back was the maroon and cream check. She'd had me buy safety pins to hold it all together. They were as large as a baby's diaper pins, but bent to go through the layers with some ease. Odd looking pins, but as with so many objects in this new quilting world, made to serve a purpose.

Lena had agreed to be my machine quilter. She was ready to go back to the quilt cabin and do it on the longarm machine.

No way was I hand quilting this, I had neither the time, nor the expertise.

Chapter 38

An Unnamed Quilt—Early October

I was learning to know Dan better. Also rolling around in my mind was the possibility of making a quilt for a new baby that a friend is having. A small one.

My quilt was nearly finished. Lena had returned the machine quilted body to me less than a week after I handed it off to her. She threw me a curve when she gave it back, saying, "What its name?"

I hadn't the slightest idea what she was talking about.

She must have understood my quizzical look. "Your quilt. This one, the one you and your Aunt Sophie made. You should name it."

"Never thought of it."

"Well, do. Naming your creation is part of it. This isn't an already named pattern, so you must give it life. A suggestion of what it's about, or represents, or whatever whimsy strikes your fancy."

I paid her and took the quilt home to my sewing room. It sat overnight while I absorbed that it only needed the binding to be ready to show. Next morning was Saturday and I called Dan to come over and help me with it. I didn't need his help, but I was becoming quite fond of his presence.

Coffee was ready when he arrived with the last of the summer fruits, a jar of blackberry jelly from his mother and a loaf of herb and grain bread he'd bought at the Farmer's Market. I had some boiled eggs in the fridge. He sliced the bread and made toast while I set the kitchen table. Everything we did seemed to go so easy. He was wearing a green plaid Pendleton shirt and Levi's, cowboy boots, and his hair was rumpled. He is a handsome one.

After breakfast I took the folded quilt to the one place in the house large enough for me to spread it out. Holding the edges we laid it loosely on my bed and stood back.

"That is rather spectacular," Dan said.

"Do you think the red edge is too flashy? Magda talked me into making it mine and I'm more flamboyant than Aunt Sophie."

"I like it. I really do." I'd left it with Lena before Dan and I really got in each other's pockets as we were now.

But we'd not been in each other's beds, yet.

I had deliberately brought Dan, into my bedroom. Still, I felt fumbly.

My side of the quilt had large rumples that I reached over to pull straight. Dan reached across from his side with both arms extended, smoothing past the middle. Our hands bumped.

He grasped my fingers, holding me to the bent-across-the-bed position. "Hey! It's okay."

He had to know I was nervous, skittish that he would take advantage of where we were, while hoping that he would.

But, this was our bed, mine and Roger's.

I could see the desire in Dan's eyes, and feel it in myself.

He released my hands. We stood straight on either side of the bed with the quilt between us, looking at each other. I hoped he couldn't see the flush I could feel warming my face.

"It's just…"

"This is your marriage bed."

I made another swipe at the quilt. "Yes."

"I have an idea." He came round the end of the bed to stand by me. "You say you will finish the quilt tonight, doing the what-do-you-call it?"

"Binding."

He put his arms around me and kissed me, a long deep kiss that took my breath. We pressed together. He ran his hands across my back, pulling me even closer. "You need a new bed. I need for you to have a new bed. You could donate this one to one of the charities. If you want." He was being very careful.

We both took deep breaths and stepped apart. I started folding the quilt. He went to the other side. We did it together.

He handed it to me, and I held it close to my chest. "Sounds good to me. This bed has a lotta miles on it and I'm ready for a new one.

"I'm gonna be spending the day with this. Get it finished. Tomorrow, I'll go shopping."

He started to speak.

"By myself.

"I'll let you know when I'm done…with the bed, and the quilt, too. You can come see."

He started to speak as we left my bedroom.

I ran over the top of his words, "It'll be a surprise."

As soon as he left I sat myself down in my sewing chair, and called Magda.

"Hello, Annie!"

"Magda. I'm in the home stretch."

"Wonderful. See, I knew you could do it."

"Not without you, and Lena, I couldn't have."

"Will you finish the binding with hand sewing? Or machine sewing?"

"By hand, of course. Only way I know to hide the seams out of sight. Mostly."

"Good. Of course whatever you do is your business, but I prefer the hand work for finishing, myself.

"Have you picked up the entry forms for the show?"

"No. Haven't even thought of it."

"No problem. I can get them in the mail this next week. Be sure to send them back as soon as possible. Lena and I have your back but it's good to get it entered on time. We have to figure space and placement, you know."

"What do you hear from Sam?"

"Oh, that Sammy." Her voice softened, dropped the business tone, became more dreamy. "I'm going down this week to pick him up. We've been back and forth since you were here. I went down and we stayed in Sophie's Cabins for a few days. That sweetie, he served me honeydew melon and toast for breakfast, I made us lunch, and we ate out nearly every night."

"How long were you there?"

"Not long. A week. I got a quilt made for our bed. Left it there for other people. Just a simple squares thing. Black and white. Teri wants me to make more, so when I have the show over, I'll play with that. Good to have work, and the beach is an inspiring place."

215

"Will the Willamina quilter have her beach quilt in the show?"

"Oh, yes. That's why you were interested in us in the first place. Judy will be showing it, for sure." We left it at that, as I wasn't sure how long "Sammy" would be staying at Magda's.

I told Magda about deciding to buy a new mattress, giving her the little bit of lowdown on Dan that I was ready to share. I knew she'd tell Sam. She could bridge my information to the family, and I could avoid a direct inquisition.

As for naming the quilt, I was having an idea but it wasn't firmed down yet. I needed to talk more with Sam. After all, it was his mother's quilt.

Had been.

Chapter 39

A New Bed

I took some days saying goodbye to my old bed, moving furniture around, putting up new curtains. Then I went shopping. I bought a new mattress and, in the same store, an oak bed frame with a wide, flat, headboard.

It cost a pretty penny but was worth it. Deeper than my old one which meant new sheets of good cotton, black and white stripes. Four pillowcases to match. New pillows. I squashed and fluffed every pillow, inhaled the fresh smell of my new linens. A thick, fluffy new comforter of a snazzy black and white check. Liberation linens.

The store delivered the new, and took away the old. Dan was there to help me. We put together the frame, put on the mattress, and helped each other make the bed. On my side I tucked with hospital corners. On his side he did military corners. We snapped the blankets on quick. Time to embrace the new.

That we did with gusto. We finished the bed making, and then, as if we'd been waiting all our lives to make love to each other, proceeded to tear it up.

We kicked off our shoes. The touch of his hands set me on fire. I pulled off his shirt, then his pants, while he stripped off my blouse and jeans. In our unders we tumbled onto the bed.

Dan played his fingers over the tiny goosebumps on the tops of my breasts. "We must warm you up." He stroked the chilly bumps with his tongue. He rolled me onto my belly, unhooked the closures on my bra, dropped it to the floor. He rolled me over again, exposing my breasts to his touch.

His urgency inflamed me as his hands explored the swell of my breasts, my belly, reached to play with the elastic of my panties. Everywhere he touched, my body lifted to his palms, his fingers. He kissed where he touched, his tongue moving smoothly over my nipples. I grabbed him by the ribs, feeling his muscles ripple as I stroked.

He moved slow and gentle while desire built within me. I tugged at his shorts. He lifted his hips to help me, took a few seconds to fit himself with a condom, then pulled off my panties. We waited no longer.

With him inside me I wanted to move, but now he stopped and raised himself on his elbows to look into my eyes, then as I whispered, urgently, "Dan," he began to shift until we were equally lost in sensation and finally, mutual explosion.

I lay warm and naked beside him, feeling my body zinging with peace. Cooling, I reached to lift the blanket. He pulled up his side. We tucked up under the covers, arms entwined, looking with wonder at each other.

"Well, hello, Miss Annie," he whispered. "So nice to know you."

"Mmm." I had no strength for talking. I traced the planes of his face, his lips, over his eyelids to close his eyes. With satisfied sighs his breathing slowed, and he slept. I watched him for a few minutes, pulled gently at his hair, kissed his quiet lips, ran my hand over the length of his body down to the round of his butt.

Prince Charming found his way onto the bed, walked over us, did a bit of purr-purr and pat-pat at my shoulder. Moving to the curve of my back, he tucked in close, settled down.

Cozy, I fell into my own deep sleep.

When we woke, moving and shifting again, Prince jumped off the bed. Dan laughed.

Feeling my inner thermostat rise again, I said, "My turn, Danny boy."

He smiled. "Oh, you must have your way. I won't even try to stop you."

I began a gentle massage of his back, shutting my eyes while I traced the lines of muscle in his shoulder, upper back, down through his legs. He was every bit as tasty as I'd thought he'd be, a lovely, strong body.

Sated once more, we slept.

When we woke we were both were full of energy, needing to move, to walk, to drive somewhere, together. "The beach!" he said. "You've told me about Sophie's Cabins, I want to sleep with you there, with the sounds of the ocean close, and you in my arms."

I called ahead. There was one cabin open.

"It's yours," Teri said. "Bring your coat with a hood. We've got a stiff breeze blowing. It's still got a little warmth in it, but not much. Might even spit rain.

"I'll make sure Sam's got some wood there for the fire. You might want to stop in town and pick up dinner before you come. There's a good chips place in town.

"We're busy tonight with the football game. The weather's iffy but you know, that won't stop 'em. Connor's starting, first time in a game. Frankly, I don't know who's more excited, Dave or Connor. Maybe you can stop in before you leave tomorrow?"

I was glad they'd all be busy. We weren't planning to socialize.

We showered together, nearly sidetracking our trip, but I stayed on task. I packed in minutes, filled Prince's water and food bowls, promised him we'd be back by tomorrow night. We stopped by Dan's mother's house by the river. While he changed clothes and stuffed an overnight bag with clean underwear and toilet articles, his mother and I sat in her living room, drinking hot tea.

By now I'd met her several times and liked her forthright and accepting manner. Her hair was dyed a soft red, her eyes were a lighter brown than his, carrying now a knowing look as she watched him rush around. At seventy-two she was retired but, from her son's reports, busier than ever with volunteering at the library and the animal shelter.

She switched to the subject of Dan. "I expect he'll be even busier now, and Lord knows, he's always on the go. I'm glad you two are taking some time to play at the beach." I finished my tea and we left.

Teri was right about the weather, and then some. By the time we got there the wind was whipping around the cabin. Sam had left the key under the mat, so we didn't even have to talk to anybody.

I set the food we'd picked up in town on the table by the picture window that faced the ocean, searched the drawers and cupboards for table settings and glasses, while Dan worked at the wood stove. He soon had a fire going to take away the room's damp. We weren't feeling the cold much anyway, carrying our own heat as we were. It could've been an igloo and us naked and we wouldn't have been bothered by the chill.

By the time we sat to eat, it was sunset, with no sun to

be seen but enough daylight to make a lovely black and white silhouette of Haystack Rock looming in the shadows of swirling sand and fog. Rain had replaced the fog, making a cocoon of our cabin.

Dan doused his fish and chips liberally with vinegar. "I learned to eat it this way in England," he said. "Now it's not authentic without the bite of malt vinegar. I like to salt it first, then the vinegar, then the lemon over all."

With my permission, he splashed vinegar on my food. I liked the zest.

"I think it's a law that if you're going to eat authentic English fish and chips you must have hot tea."

"But the English do it with milk. Not for me. Milk is for babies, and that we certainly ain't." He pointed his vinegary fry at me.

I snapped it from his hands, ate it.

I barely had time to clean up dinner before we jumped into bed and continued our education. Dan got up once to feed the fire. When he came back to bed his bare legs brushed mine, once again inflaming my need. I had never felt like this before. Pure lust that at one moment had me gasping, the next wanting to dominate him, and then to submit. We went from deep sleep to hyper awake, and passion spent, back to deep sleep.

In the morning I was awakened by knocking. I fumbled into my robe and went to the door.

Sam stood there with two cups of hot coffee on a tray. "When you're awake, come on up and have breakfast. We have news for you." He left.

Ah, well, we could use the break. I took the tray to Dan, and we watched the ocean while we drank. Seagulls flew against the wind. The rain had become a light mist. The fire in the woodstove had gone out, and the coolness of the room finally energized us to scramble out of bed.

We showered separately, as the stall was too small for two. I gloried in the luxury of the hot water, knowing that in 1918 Aunt Sophie had no such indoor benefit, just a roughed-in, outdoor affair that her brothers had rigged up.

Dressed and out, we struggled through the wind the short way to the beach, "To work up an appetite," we told each other, as we hiked all the way to the Rock. I stared at it while I held my scarf tight to my ears.

We didn't stay long before going back to the cabin, and then up to the Old Place where Sam had lived nearly the whole of his life.

"Sorry," Dan said to Sam, as he opened the door. "We forgot the cups."

Sam hurried us into the door, out of the damp wind. "Well, well. You must be Dan. I've heard of you. Put your coat here." He pointed to the pegs by the door that were put there by his father, David Smithers.

I hurried to introduce them, "Dan, meet my cousin Sam, Sam, my, um, friend, Dan Dee."

Sam tilted his head at Dan's name, as if maybe he'd not heard right, but only said, "Glad to meetcha, and don't worry about the cups." He turned back to me after shaking hands with Dan. "I see from the booking that you are leaving today. Short trip, huh?"

"We wanted to take a walk on the beach, and I wanted you all to meet."

Sam led us to the dining room where Dave and Connor were already at the table, Teri was by the stove in the kitchen.

Connor leaped up to say hello to me and to look sharply at Dan. "So, you must be the new guy, huh?"

"Connor!" Teri said.

"What?" he asked, all innocence.

"That would be me," Dan said, as serious as could be, "Where do I sit?"

Dave laughed and the short spot of tension dissolved as Dan laughed, too. "I'm Dan Dee. Who would you be, the old guy?"

Connor pulled back, and blushed.

Teri had come from the kitchen to meet Dan, now she laughed. "Oh, good one."

Connor sulked for a minute while I introduced Dan to Dave and Teri. When I kissed him on the top of his head, he ducked away.

"This one is my precocious cousin, third cousin I believe. He has an interest in bugs, is raising cockroaches. A special kind of roach."

The kid came out of his short funk, "Hissing Cockroaches, Annie. But that's a was, I don't have time for that now." He pushed out his chest, "I'm a football player now, made a touchdown last night. Gonna have to be working at that now, eating right, learning plays, like that."

"You're a quarterback?" Dan said.

Teri set a plate of pancakes on the table, "No, thank God, he's not even in the running for quarterback."

"I'm an inside linebacker," Connor said.

Dave was smiling, proud.

"But he did make a good play last night," Teri continued. "Pulled out the winning play, a touchdown in the last minute, breaking a tie that had threatened to keep us later, shivering in the stadium. I have to admit, it was a thrill. I still don't like it though."

"Aw, Mom. I'm all right." He grinned at her, a teenage boy knowing he had his mother's heart, and of course having no understanding of her fear. I felt the same way she did.

"I agree with your mom, it's a dangerous sport, too much chance to damage that precious brain of yours, heaven knows you don't have much to play with."

I'd no sooner gotten the words out of my mouth than Dan said, "Good show! Maybe we can come down and catch a game sometime. I played in high school and college, too."

I guess I glared at him, 'cause he amended, "But they're right, it can be hard on your body."

Connor's jealousy disappeared in a flash, as he served himself, barely paying attention to what he was doing. Clearly, to him Dan had potential. "What did you play? Who with?" Between bites he added, "You look all right. Must be pretty smart to get Cousin Annie to hang around with you."

"High school. OSU. Inside linebacker, mostly. Like you," Dan said in answer to Connor's question. "I don't know about how smart I am, but I was lucky in football. Either way, life seems to be like that, you just gotta take your chances." Here he smiled at me. "Like asking out the pretty ones, even if you don't think you have a chance. Sometimes you get smacked down, sometimes you make a touchdown."

Connor blushed again, which Dan ignored. "Seems I'm making a winning play. You never know, but hey! You gotta try, right?"

Dave and Connor moved over into his camp, then and there.

Teri sat down at the table. "Men!" she said, with a shake of her head.

I was nodding in agreement when Sam said, "Speaking of women," which made us listen. "Have you talked to Magda lately?"

"Not for a couple of days, why?" I didn't tell him I'd spent most of the last few days either buying a bed or being in one, not talking to anybody but Dan.

"I'm looking for a ride to Magda's."

"We could take you today, but we're going to be on our way in just a couple hours."

"I need more time than that. See, I've got to gather some things together, more than I'd take for a weekend." He had a funny smile on his face.

"Sam! What are you telling me? What are you doing?"

"See, that's what I'm trying to tell you. Magda and I wanted to tell you together. She's called you a couple times this week to set up a meeting but, the only person answering your phone is the machine. Now, I know why." This he said smugly as he grinned at the both of us.

"Tell me what? She must have called while I was out and I never noticed the light." I felt like I'd been caught out. How embarrassing in front of Connor, and everybody.

"I'm moving in with Magda. And she's moving in with me. We're taking over one of Sophie's Cabins and making it ours for when we live here. Half the time we'll live here, and half the time we'll live in Willamina."

"What great news! When does this start?"

"Already. Done. I'm here getting our place nailed down for winter, chimney needs cleaned, for one thing. Getting a guy in today to do them all so it's good you're leaving."

"Which one?" I said.

"Which one, what? Oh, which cabin for us? The one Mom and her brothers lived in. Not much of the old left but the basic construction. We modernized it years ago. Added on a section. It's the biggest cabin, and my favorite." He stood up, and took his plate to the kitchen. "You should stop by and see Magda on your way home."

"As a matter of fact, that's just what we're doing," Dan said.

"Yes," I said. "I'm done with the quilt and I'll leave it with Magda for the show. And I want to introduce Dan to her. I'm calling ahead this morning, so your news wouldn't have been a secret much longer."

"Lord, girl, it's not been a secret. You've just been on another planet, or something." He broke off as he saw Connor closely following our exchange. "Anyway. Come by the cabin on your way out, I'll show you what I've done. And you can tell Magda that everything is just about ready. I've had some legal things to do, too."

I was flabbergasted. "You two getting married?"

"No. Doing a thing called Domestic Partnership. Formalizing what's hers, what's mine, and what will be ours. Make everything clear."

He looked at Dave and Teri. "Time to get some things legalized. I'm giving up my legal part in this place, turning it over to the kids here. It would've gone to them anyway. This just gets it done, sooner. We'll take over that one cabin and the kids will still rent out the others. We'll get a percentage. Magda and I have enough, and everybody will know what's theirs. Legally."

"So, when are ya leaving today? Want me to call Maggie?"

"All right. Let me know when we come by your cabin if she

226

can't see us today. I can always come back by tomorrow. We've still got time before the show."

On the way out we stopped by Sam's and Magda's new place. Dave and Connor were there, helping Sam tighten up the place for winter. Sam led us into his new place. In the front room I saw, sitting on the coffee table, Roger's ship model that Sam had taken home with him to finish. It felt so right that it was here; a tiny, unacknowledged piece of anxiety within me, dissolved. "Perfect," I said to Sam.

"I thought so," he said. "Come on through, here." We followed him to where they'd opened up an unfinished third bedroom. It had a large window and they had added shelves that Magda needed. "Magda likes light. This'll be her sewing room."

I could tell Sam was proud of their work.

"We added this room on several years ago. Magda's gonna love the view here." He waved his hand to indicate the ocean and the Rock in the distance. "She's gonna make new curtains for our place, and she'll be making quilts for all the cabin beds. Ought to keep her busy for a while."

Connor was hanging over the roof edge when we were on our way out. "Here to check out the old folks love nest?"

Sam called up to Dave. "Could you whack that sassy kid of yours, talking disrespectful?"

Dave stuck his head around the corner of the chimney. "I don't know. I was thinking of making a new sign for your cabin, hanging it by the door, The Love Nest."

"You're lucky I don't feel like coming up there and giving you both what for." To us he added, loud enough for them to hear, "You just can't get good help anymore. It's hard what an old man has to put up with."

"Hey," yelled Connor, "You best be respectful of the help. I'm standing over your bedroom and with just a few shuffles of my feet you could be waking up in a puddle some morning. See who has the last laugh."

While Dan and I laughed at their banter, he reached in his pocket and brought out some cash, that he tried to hand to Sam.

"You're with our sweetie here, you don't ever pay."

"Hmm, I just hit the jackpot. I thought all I'd got was the prettiest gal in Oregon, but I can freeload at the beach, too."

"Oh, don't worry, we'll be putting you to work. You know the old saying, 'No such thing as a free lunch.' Annie and you are welcome anytime. Just let Teri know ahead of time."

He walked us out to our car. "What you can do is stop by the material store here in town and pick up some quiltin' doodad for Magda, tell her it's from me, that I earned it from my riches as a beach bum. Or whatever. She's waiting for ya so you best be going."

I hugged him, kissed his cheek. "You old fool. I can't tell you how happy I am for you. And Magda."

There was a chilly rain coming down when we arrived at her place. She had the front door open before we were halfway through the rose arbor. "Get in here, it's cold out there. Isn't it nice how you don't get thorned now?" She ushered us into the house. "You must be Dan. Just put the bag there, on the table. I'll be looking at it soon enough. I've got some tea and just-made banana bread, ready in the sun room."

I handed her the packet of buttons I'd bought at the fabric store. "Here, from Sam," I said.

She nodded and set them on a shelf, "He's so thoughtful." And clever, I thought, remembering the effort I'd taken to fill his request. She waved to Dan to follow her.

I took Dan's jacket with mine and hung them from the coat rack while Magda took him through to the sun room. When I came in she'd already set him down at the small table with tea and a plate with four slices of the bread.

Dan got up from the table to pull out my chair. I sat, feeling the sense of comfort as a constant here. Easy to see why Sam was so ready to start sharing it with her. Beyond the windows the world was a rainy mess, as my mother used to say. It only enhanced the close comfort of the room.

I took a drink of the hot tea, before biting into the bread, "Sampson told us about you two. How exciting!"

She cradled her cup in her hands, smiling widely. "He did, huh? Yup, pretty big thing. Changing my whole life. His too. Are you surprised?"

"Not at you two, but, yes, this is big. Are you ready to share your life again, so soon? What do the quilt club ladies say? Well, heck, how do you feel about making so many changes all at once?"

Dan gave Magda a questioning look as he reached for another piece of bread. She pushed the plate closer to him, "Take as much as you want. I've been on a spree the last couple of days. Making bread, muffins. I can't eat it all."

To me she said, "Getting ready for Sammy, I guess. Been a long time since I had anybody 'sides myself to care for. Feels good. I want to bake and spruce up things, wash the curtains, hang the rugs over the fence and beat the old dust out of them." She looked at the rain beyond the window. "Like Spring cleaning, but here we are, moving into winter almost. So to answer your question, yes, I'm happy. Excited. Some scared. When he asked me if we could share our lives I wasn't too surprised. We'd started doing that soon after he come up here

229

with you. But to make it real, not just play-acting. Feels right."

The bread plate was empty again. "Why don't you bring us some more, Dan? It's already cut, just waiting."

He left quick enough.

She lowered her voice. "How's it going with you two? He's a good looking one, strong too, I think. He's got that look in his eye that I like in a man. Steady."

Dan came back and set the refreshed plate on the table. He poured himself more tea before putting another piece on his plate.

"Who would've guessed, us two, so single when we met at the Fair? Well," she amended, "I wasn't single, but I certainly was alone. Now here we are, all coupled up and getting cozy."

"Sam and I are two very lucky guys." Dan said, around another bite of the bread.

Magda and Sam would be working together with the Guild and the Wrestlers to set the place up. "We have a full Art Walk, a real event to bring people in. Even though we're a small town, we have a lot of talent here. Your entrance fee gives you a chance to win our Guild quilt. It's a dandy this year."

She eyed Dan. "If you could help with the setting up, you can meet Big Juan. Now there's an experience." She chuckled. "Lena and Big Juan are becoming quite an item."

"Let's go look at your quilt. I saw it when Lena was working on it, but I'm anxious to see what it looks like, done."

On the way to her workroom, she said, "Your boy Len is going to give a talk at our show this year."

"About his quilt?"

"*Tumbling Blocks*? No. He's calling his talk, 'Extreme Sewing, a Matter of Life and Death.'"

"He didn't want us to advertise the talk, but we've put it on the paper flyers around town. And Sunshine put it on our website. Kinda upset him. Lena begged him to let us keep it in. She thinks it'll be a good draw. Once a day, at two o'clock.

"Interesting," was all I could say.

Together we opened my quilt onto the large table in her sewing room.

"Oh, my. You done good, girl. It's wonderful. The checks and stripes give it just the touch of snazzy all that plainness needed." She patted it, pulling off a loose thread, used scissors to snip off a hanging thread. "Never pull a thread that is connected."

"You're not going to win a prize. Too many tucks and gathers, but you've got the eye. You thinking of selling it?"

"Sell it? Oh, no. Never. I have the perfect place for it."

I had a plan for the quilt but I wasn't ready to share it, or its name, with her yet.

She read the signature I'd embroidered at the bottom of the quilt: Sophie Elm, 1976, Annie Straw, 2010. "Your first quilt. But I'm betting, not your last."

I wasn't ready to take that bet, thinking of the baby quilt I was working up in my mind.

Chapter 40

My Gift

Day One of the Show, Friday

This was a most interesting day in my life, starting with waking up in my bed with Dan's arm over my back, my bottom curled into the cavity between his legs and chest, his gentle snoring in my ear. I'm glad for the sweet beginning, because it wasn't long before the day began to rumble.

I made oatmeal in the microwave, bowls too small, the oatmeal boiled over. I made toast in the oven, burned it. Forgot to put the water in the coffee maker when I turned it on and nothing happened, except it got hot. That was bad, as I really needed coffee. In the cupboard, telltale marks of cat lick on the butter. I never find the cupboard door open, just his tongue marks, so he must close it again, too.

Dan took over, cut off the cat licks, scrambled eggs for us in the good butter, saying no disparaging things about the Prince. Made more toast, poured a couple glasses of grapefruit juice for us. Even cleaned up the oatmeal. Added water to the coffee pot and served it all up with a kiss. Good thing I had food to hold me up through the morning.

My cell rang just before I stepped into the shower. It was

Magda. "Annie, where are you? You said you would be here early with your quilt. It's seven already."

For gosh sakes, they'd hung the show yesterday morning, as the trial run. Couldn't leave it up because of the wrestling match last night, so had taken it down yesterday afternoon and re-hung it this morning.

"The spot for your quilt is empty. We open in two hours. We can't still be hanging it while people are coming in. Already enough that I had to deal with Big Juan so early. He and Lena are smitten and foolish. They made sure that I knew he won his match last night. Like I care. They're a lot to mess with so early in the morning.

"Sammy doesn't do so well with him. I'm seeing a side of your Sam..."

Your Sam?

"...that I'm not happy with. Get your Dan here. He can put out these fires. Get a move on!"

I'm not the only nervous one, here. Perhaps the unflappable Magda is feeling pressure, too?

"Okay Magda, we're moving as fast as we can. I've got the quilt all rolled up, ready to hang."

Gosh, the pressure. Who knew I'd be so nervous. And then I heard a car. I pushed the curtain aside and saw in my driveway, the Thunderbird. Len was driving, with a woman beside him. The top was up, I couldn't see her face.

Len knocked at my door while she stayed in the car. Dan answered. That put Len off, and his attitude carried through the bathroom window.

"Where's Annie? Aren't you that fire guy?"

Dan now knew all about Len, I'd told him our history and how he'd come back into my life. He was easy with it all.

233

"Annie's getting ready for the show. Yeah, I'm the 'fire guy'. You need something?"

"It's private, if you don't mind. I'll go on to the show, talk to her then. You will tell her I was here, won't you? And that I want to talk to her?"

"Of course. She can call you on her cell while we're on the road. We'll be on our way here in just a little bit."

"No need. I'll see her at the show." He started away, then turned, "So, you'll be there, too?"

"Wouldn't miss it."

"Great." But he didn't sound like it he thought it would be great.

"Does your friend want to come in? Or you? We have coffee."

"Her name is Luanne." He ignored the invite. "I'd appreciate it if you'd be nice to her today. Be the first time she's seen my work, and meets my co-workers."

"Co-workers?"

"You know what I mean. Fellow artists." He started away again, "So I guess I'll see the both of you there?" he asked again.

"Yes, we'll both be there."

With that he left and I let out the breath I didn't know I'd been holding. Lord, why did I ever get mixed up with him again.

In the shower I thought about what I'd worked up last night to be added to the quilt, and smiled. I'd had a Good Idea, I hoped. Magda sounded almost cranky this morning. She might not be up for any surprises at the show.

There'd also be a surprise that Len didn't know about. That Katie Heap person who has a T-Bird too, would be there today. I'm looking forward to meeting her.

And I'm wondering how Magda's friends feel about Sam moving in. She'd never answered that question the day we'd stopped at her...their...place. I don't know what she's told them, she's been so busy with the show. I'm wondering if they will be happy for her, or scandalized that she's sharing house with a man, so quick.

We arrived in plenty of time to check into our motel and get to the show a full half hour before the doors opened, expecting to find a parking place, easy, but there were cars parked all up and down the street, and the next door parking lot was full too. We parked way up the street.

People were lined up just beyond the front door. Wow, this was a bigger draw than I'd expected. Lena and a guy dressed like a wrestler cartoon in skin tight orange pants and a sleeveless green and orange striped t-shirt met us outside the door. Had to be Big Juan. They were pinning up advertising for that night's Wrestling Match. I heard him say, "Listen to me, my sweet, one of your quilter gals took this down. They don't like it that we are here. They think we're a scandal to the show."

"Oh, Honey Buns, how can you think that? They all love you, like I do." She patted the muscular arm that was holding the poster in place while she pushed in tacks.

"No, not like you do," he said.

The wrestler giggled. Lena the tough giggled.

Lena noticed us and whispered to him. She and I said hello and hugged. Big Juan held out his hand to Dan while nodding to me. "Mrs. Straw? And you must be Mr. Dee?"

Dan shook hands with him. "Yes, I am. And you are?" He knew who this was, he'd already told me he didn't like the idea of calling him "Big". This was his way of finding out what to call him.

"Juan. I'm on tonight. This is me." The poster had him pictured in a grapple with another guy. The bold lettering announced their names and time of the matches, last night and tonight. "Will you two be here?"

Lena said, "Juan won last night. He was wonderful. Nobody can beat him."

I nodded to her but answered him, "That depends on how today goes. We're staying over with Magda and Sam. We might be too tired to make it."

Dan must have seen Lena's pleading look. "We'll do our best to come. I used to wrestle some in high school, kinda get a kick outa watching you guys. It's a real art, doing what you do and not killing each other. Pretend wrestling."

Big Juan's eyes flared.

I grabbed Dan's arm. "Hey, we can talk about it later. Magda wants us in there. Right now." I gave his arm an extra tug as the air filled with testosterone. What is it with these guys?

The entry was a double door setup with enough space between the inner and outer doors for one to close before the other is opened. It keeps wind and rain from blowing in. Once we were between the two doors I whispered, "I can't believe you said that."

"What? Just speaking truth. I do admire them, at least their physical abilities to slam each other around, and no one dies." He pushed the inner door open.

Color was everywhere. Quilts hung in rows across the floor of the big room, were mounted high on the walls. Tables at the front and back were piled with potholders, table runners, trivets, other quilted items. At the far end was a large, beautiful quilt in a frame standing high on a table. It was the star quilt I'd worked on at the quilting bee. Someone with a ticket to the show would win it. I hoped it would be me.

Magda whipped over to us. I didn't know she could walk that fast. She took the bag holding my quilt. I was busy staring at the kaleidoscope of colors and designs. Different from the State Fair where quilts had been lining the room. Here they *were* the room.

Magda took Dan with her to help hang my quilt, while I stood, bedazzled by flowers and squares and triangles, a tsunami of geometry. I needed to follow Magda and Dan but I was distracted. *I'll just take a moment here...* Pinned to each creation was a tag with the name of the quilt, of the maker and an explanation of the idea behind the design. If it was for sale, the price was there, and if not, to whom it belonged. Below the information, in big letters, was: PLEASE DO NOT TOUCH! HOLD THIS TAG TO LOOK AT THE BACK.

I was reminded of Lena's admonishment to "Never, never, touch a quilt." I saw now what she meant. In a public setting like this the oil from the fingers of so many people would mark it, and in the long run, damage the fabric.

No lookers or customers were in the room yet, just members of the guild. Sunshine came over to me and said, "Hey, let me show you your Len's quilt. It's smashing."

"He's not 'my Len,'" I said, protesting uneasily as I followed her down an aisle "Only a second."

"No matter. Over here." She led me to the far wall at the back of the room where his *Tumbling Blocks* was standing alone, hanging from a frame made especially for it. I liked it. The 3-D design is a dazzling trick to the eye.

"Is he here?" I said.

"No, he brought it in yesterday. Haven't seen him yet today. You know he's bringing in another item to put right here. We'll make room when he comes. Going to give a short talk about it, at two I think."

I already knew that. I was thinking about my quilt and Magda. I wanted to be with Magda and Sam when they hung it. I excused myself and found her, with Sam, in a middle row. Why did I think he might be elsewhere?

He was standing by an empty space in the line. Dan was there too. He had his hands tight on the end of the bag, holding it taut as Magda pulled out the quilt.

"Hey! Just in time," Dan said. A small crowd of the Guild women and their helpers gathered around us. The doors had yet to open.

I held up my hand. "I have something special here to add to the info about who made it, and all. It doesn't belong to me anymore, don't know if it ever did. Magda and Sampson, this is my present to you." I took out the piece of paper I'd printed up. Dan stood by me as I fished out tape and attached it the sheet.

"Sam, you come over here, by Magda." I read while they listened.

This quilt, Sweethearts, *belongs to* Sampson Smithers *and* Magda Buler,
to honor their relationship. Gifted to them by its makers:
his mother, Sophie Elm, and their friend, Annie Elm Straw. November 2012

Magda listened with her hand over her mouth. Sam held her other hand like he wasn't quite sure what to think, to do.

When I finished, they were grinning ear to ear. I took a

nice photo.

"Gosh," said Magda, "I guess the secret's out now!"

"As it should be." Sam gave her a quick kiss on her blushing cheek. He kissed my cheek, too. First time ever. "Thank you so much, Annie. I never guessed."

"Me neither," said Magda. "So we can take it home when the show is over?"

"Yes indeed. It's yours."

"Guess you'll have to make one for your bed, now." She gave Sam the clips to attach *Sweethearts* to the line. "Next time you make a quilt for show, you must sew a hanger on the back of it to slide a roller through.

"Whoops, the doors are open. Here they come."

Chapter 41

Lethal Lena

I watched as several of Magda's friends read the info on our quilt. Some were surprised to learn of her and Sam. A couple were quietly disapproving, and whispered, "Not married. I just don't think what she's doing is right. So soon." But most demanded to meet this Sampson person, and congratulated them. She ran the gauntlet of the town's thoughts with few scratches. No scandal.

The morning's biggest source of excitement was Lena. Most people who came in were looking for quilts, but an enthusiastic number of them were looking for "That woman, Lena."

I must have had a look of authority because one of them, a sweet young thing with dyed, bright red hair, wearing a black tee covered with sequins and holey jeans with crazy quilt patches came up to me and asked, "Could you tell me where Lena's quilts are? Is she here?"

"Sure. Follow me." I took Dan's hand to lead us through the crowd to where a line had formed in front of her quilts.

From our place a row over I could hear what they were saying.

"Can you believe?"

"She killed her friend's husband, you know."

"Don't forget the bear!"

"In self-defense. The man, not the bear."

"Lethal Lena."

"When will she come in?" Apparently none of them realized they had already seen her at the door.

I decided to warn the women at the cash table about what was going on. Heads began to turn as Lena's name began to sound above the crowd noise. I looked to where the buzz was loudest just as Lena and Big Juan strolled into the room, arms linked.

They were wrapped up in each other, and didn't notice the attention they were drawing. She led Juan to the first row of quilts, which happened to be where Dan and I were standing. She took a moment from her absorption with Juan to say hello to us, then went back to the reason she'd brought him here, to show him the finer points about quilting. She pulled one out to show him the stitching.

I realized she wasn't aware that the crowd was closing around them when I heard her say, "Here, count these. Mariah has a deft hand, no fewer than ten stitches to an inch, ever. We put her right here in the first row. She and I are the only ones to do all our stitching by hand—well at least sewing together the quilt sandwich. Remember what I told you, how it's not a quilt if it doesn't have the three layers?"

He nodded, as if he was hanging onto her every word.

The attention of the crowd was beginning to alarm me. Lena let go of the quilt to put her hand in Juan's, still talking as they edged on to the next piece.

"...unless it's an Art Quilt. We have different qualifications, there."

I moved with the crowd, right behind the red haired girl who was so close to Lena that she was mashed against her back. Juan gave Red Hair a *Back off* look while Lena said, "Excuse me," to her, and gave her a small push.

Turning back to Juan she went on. "Now this one is by my dear Magda. See how cleverly she has matched and contrasted the colors? This is called Log Cabin." She put an arm out to stop Red Hair and her friends who were crushed so close that Lena and Juan could barely move. "It's an old fashioned pattern with several variations on how it's put together."

I was finally close enough to reach over and tap Lena on the shoulder. She looked up and saw me waving my hand to show her the crowd closing in on them. She said to him, "Fans, Big. Look, you've gathered a crowd."

His chest puffed up. "It's usual. Comes with the territory." He turned to the man nearest him. "I'd prefer to not give autographs right now, I'm with my lady."

The guy gave him a funny look. "I don't know who you are. I just want to talk to her."

"Me? Whatever for?" Lena was clearly baffled and stared at him, her eyes big.

"If you'd just sign this I'd appreciate it." He held out a small autograph album and a pen.

I could only stand and watch, astounded.

She shrank closer to Juan, "Whatever for? Are you crazy?"

One of the women behind her said, "No, honey. We just appreciate you. You're a hero."

"What?"

"I read about you in the paper." She held out a page of newsprint, pointed at a photo of Lena coming from the courthouse with her lawyer. "The way you took care of that man who was attacking you. That took courage. I'm sure you weren't the first one he's tried to hurt."

Another woman said, "The whole story's on the Internet. You took care of that bear, too. Nobody better mess with you." She pulled a notebook from her purse. "Could I have your autograph, too?"

Lena clung to Juan's arm. "I don't think so. I mean, that's kind of you to want me to sign your little book, but, you're mistaken. I'm not a hero."

"But you are." A third woman stepped close, causing Lena to clutch Juan's arm tighter.

Juan instantly became her Protector. "Back off, people! You're scaring her."

The man was still holding out his album, open to an empty page. "I don't think she scares easily. Won't hurt her to sign my book."

I saw the crowd surge with him as he took a step toward her.

"Hey! Didn't you hear me? I said 'Back off!'" Juan's hand shot up, flat palm out. He shoved at the guy's shoulder.

The autograph book flew one way, the pen the other. The man stumbled backwards, banged into the woman close behind him. She crashed sideways into Sam and Dan, who'd just walked up. Sam grabbed onto a pole for support and it held long enough for him and the woman to gain their feet, then it went over. Dan grabbed at it, but too late. The pole, which was supporting a whole row of quilts, fell.

The room went still. That got the attention of the Guild women. Gretchen was first there. She steadied Sam. "Now look here." She glared at the crowd, and then at the pile of color and fabric on the floor. "See what you've done!"

Sam stepped out of her grasp, "No problem. I'm okay."

"It's these crazed fans of my sweet one," Big Juan growled. "They tried pushing her around. Won't happen while I'm here."

Gretchen wasn't listening. "Gotta get these up." She took hold of the pole that had taken the quilts to the floor. "Come on, you men. Be of use here, I can't do this by myself."

Other Guild members were bumping into each other, flustered. I saw Mariah pick up a quilt, look around, and holding tight, refuse to let go when one of the men tried to take it from her. Her white-haired sister rescued a different quilt, when someone grabbed its other end. In the tugging it fell to the floor. Someone shrieked, "You stepped on my quilt!"

Dan's voice cut through the chaos. "Okay, folks, let's get a plan here. Sam, you down at this end, on this pole. Juan, you at the support on the other end. You—" He pointed at the man who'd lost his autograph book, and set off the whole debacle. "What's your name?"

"Carl."

"Carl, you get in the middle here, grab this pole. You ladies space yourselves along the sides, opposite each other. And you Lodge guys." Some men from the VFW had joined the party "Grab hold. These quilts are heavy."

We all followed his orders, mostly with a minimum of fuss.

"Good. Now, when I say lift, everybody lift. Got that?"

Juan started to lift.

"No, Juan, wait until I say, 'Lift!'" Lena had placed herself near Juan, I stood opposite her. I noticed her fans were close by, eyes gleaming while they watched their heroine.

What an opportunity, almost better than an autograph.

244

All of us bent over, ready.

A light flashed.

I looked up and there was Len. His radar was deadly. I resisted the impulse to let go of my hold on the pole and snatch the camera away from him.

He must have seen my anger, because he pointed the camera right at me and snapped off another shot.

I glared at him but didn't let go.

"Now! Lift!" As we all lifted Dan came to our end and helped Juan set his pole upright. One of the men from the Lodge did the same at the other end, while Carl stayed steady with his center support. Other people moved in and adjusted the quilts so that all were even.

"All right!" Dan stepped back.

People began to clap.

He laughed. "Hey, we all get by with a little help from our friends, right?"

The men shook hands all around, except Len who stayed off to the side, taking pictures. Juan and Carl dropped their macho stance now that they had worked in unison.

It was obvious to me that Len didn't feel a part of the team. He didn't know what to do with his feelings, so he used his camera as a shield. I almost felt sorry for him.

As we walked away from the scene of the excitement, I remembered the initial reason I'd been interested in the Willamina Quilt Show, and told Dan. "There's a special quilt I must see, that Judy has made. Of Cannon Beach. She told me about it at the quilting bee. A smaller version of one I saw at Magda's studio."

I'd learned at the quilting bee who'd made it. Judy. I found her at the pay table, and asked her where it was.

"I'll show you. Magda told me your aunt's story and that you saw my larger 'Haystack' at her studio. This came out of that one. It's an art piece."

When we got to the side wall where it hung, I stood stunned. An appliqué piece about three feet square. A mix of images sewn onto a back piece of brown that made a frame. The scene depicted in fabric and embroidery was the interior of a cabin with log walls. On a simple chair sat a woman with her back to us, looking out a window at Haystack Rock. It could have been Sophie.

The tag showed the title: *At Peace*. Beside the title tag hung the round medallion of a blue ribbon winner: Best of Show. The price was three hundred dollars.

I'd been driven by this mystery quilt to start the journey I was now on. "It's perfect. I have to have it. Consider it sold. Thank you."

Puzzled at my thanks, she answered, "I'm glad you like it, so, sure. It's yours. But let me thank you."

It had been a long morning. Dan and I left to eat at a local church advertising lunch. We had soup and sandwiches, cinnamon rolls, all handmade and served by the church women. Then we walked and drove the whole of the Art Tour, signing up at every shop or venue, hoping to win a prize. We got back just before Len's talk at two. I wouldn't miss it.

He'd set up the framed-in-glass parka on an easel. He had a good audience, including Sam and Magda. We sat in the chairs they'd saved for us. I thought I saw the woman who had been in his car this morning in the front row, but since I'd only seen the top of her head, not her face, I wasn't sure. The crowd got too big for the seating, and while someone was bringing in more chairs Len began his speech.

"The Inuit—Eskimos, to you..." He went on about their

hunting culture, and how they had expanded to the sea. "They invented the kayak to get them onto the ocean where they could harpoon the big fish, seals, walrus, whales for life sustaining blubber. Beyond calamari, or tenderized clams in butter sauce."

A few people laughed politely. "But, if the water of the Arctic, or Bering Sea splashed them they would freeze to death in minutes. So, the women made this protection, a Kamleika, cut from many pieces of seal or walrus intestine, finishing the overlapping seams with hundreds—thousands, of tiny stitches. Waterproof. The hunter put it on over his warm parka. The bottom of the jacket flared to a wide, finished hem.

"Now, for the genius. The kayak had a skin covering that was wide and loose around the cockpit. When he was in, his wife stitched him into his kayak, joining the hem of his Kamleika to the wide skirt of the cockpit. Her stitches made the waterproof seal. Brilliant.

"True life and death stitching. Any questions?"

From a man in front, "Where did you get this Kamleika? You're not an Eskimo."

"My wife's sister married into a tribe up there and when we were visiting one of the men gave it to me. Someday I'll give it to a museum."

A woman in the back asked, "How'd you learn about all this?"

"Honey, there's lots of information on the Internet. Parkas like this are in several museums. Plus, the man who gave it to me shared some of it."

He looked over the crowd, as if seeking more questions. He was looking toward one side when he suddenly appeared spooked. His eyes opened wide and his head reared up.

If I hadn't been looking at him I wouldn't have seen his reaction, because it all happened so quickly.

He took the frame from the easel, set it on the floor. "All the time I have now, folks. Thanks for listening." He stashed the easel under a nearby table, picked up the frame, and left, followed by the girl friend.

I heard someone say, "And just when I had something to ask him."

Marge came up with a woman I didn't know. "Annie, I want you to meet Katie Heap. You two have something in common. Katie, this is Annie who's been asking us about your T-Bird."

"Pleased to meet you, I'm sure, Annie. You want to know about my 'Bird, or Thunderbirds, in general?"

"Yours. I understand you're a friend of Len's?"

"Bolder?"

"Yes."

"I'm a friend of Len's wife, Linda. Len comes with the deal, but we're not particularly friends."

"She's his ex-wife."

"She's his wife."

My head was reeling. "So he lets you borrow his car?"

"This is a confusing conversation. It's not his car, it's mine. Who are you?"

"Well I used to be a friend of Len's. An old friend. I met him again at the State Fair. Later he gave me a ride in his Thunderbird."

"His car? The 'Bird?" She repeated, "That's my car. I have another one so I loaned it to him while he was at the Fair, selling his book."

"He was also showing his quilt."

"I didn't know he had any of his quilts at the Fair."

"The same one is here, in the back. He's also been taking pictures, and he just gave a talk on the Kamleika that he brought to display. But he left rather quickly."

"Oh, I did see him slither away. He was giving the talk about what?"

"His Kamleika that he got from a friend of his wife's, in the Arctic."

"Don't know about that."

"Didn't you see his—I mean, your—car outside? He was driving it this morning."

"I came with Linda in their Toyota. Left the 'Bird at their house. You saw it this morning?"

I was slow answering because I was processing Len in a Toyota. One that belonged to him and his *wife*. I don't get involved with married men. NO. I shuddered to think I'd nearly stepped into that. "At my house. He stopped by to tell me he'd be here today." No need for me to mention the woman. Not my business. "He told me he was divorced."

"No. He's a womanizer. Linda knows that. But she says she loves him. You know how that goes."

"I've heard. He'll be back tomorrow for his lecture again."

"Okay, just might be here for that. We're in town for the whole two days. I never expected so many people. Cars are parked way up the street and around. Probably why I didn't see my 'Bird.

"I think something besides quilts is fueling the interest here. The quilts are outstanding, but we have a celebrity among us."

"A celebrity? Somebody famous?"

"Depends on how you define famous. It appears that the story of Lena dispatching Magda's abusive husband made the papers and it's getting around, like, you know, on the Internet."

"I always did think that gal was meant for stardom, but I thought it would be for having fifteen stitches per inch, not killing her best friend's husband."

"She's around hanging on the arm of that wrestler guy with the orange pants. Big Juan."

"I'll watch for her. I just hope to see Len again, talk to him about 'our' car. Divorced, huh? He makes a good first impression but it doesn't hold up."

"Thanks for telling me about his quilt. Gotta see that. But first, I'm here to see the old quilt you and Magda finished."

With that I directed Katie to *Sweethearts*, and left her.

The crowd had died down from the crush and noise of people searching for Lena, and the small gathering for Len's talk. A gentle peace settled over the show, an easy hum with occasional exclamations and little squeals.

I told him about meeting with Katie, it being her car, and that Len is still married.

"The guy's a jerk. I'm don't know why you were ever with him."

"I was young. And then, well…yes, he's a jerk." I let it go at that.

Day one had been eventful way beyond what I'd expected. There was more on the night's menu. Dan and I went to our motel, "rested", and, after an early dinner, went back to the VFW building for the wrestling match. I could hardly believe we were there but was being supportive of Lena, and I must admit, too, to some curiosity.

Magda and Sam also came.

While Big Juan strutted around the ring prior to the start of the match, Lena joined his other fans in cheering him on, and put down his opponent.

I would have found it embarrassing if Dan hadn't whispered, "Ease up. This is theatre, and he's good at it. I hope the guy gives him a match."

He did. They threw each other around the ring, jumped on each other's chests, attacked from behind and pulled other dirty tricks that brought the crowd to their feet, shouting *Foul!* among other pejorative screamings.

I cringed at the thunder of the body slams, while Lena smiled. Eventually, after they'd banged into the ropes and bruised each other enough, Big Juan upended Ted The Trouncer by going in under his legs, flipping him flat on his back. Big held him there until the referee completed the count and declared him the winner.

Lena screamed in jubilation and pride.

I whispered in Dan's ear, "I've done my good deed for the year. Can we go now? Maybe pie?" He invited Sam and Magda. "Lena, want to come?" He named the only restaurant that would still be open.

"Sure, we'll meet you there." Big Juan had hardly a bruise, only a tiny Band-Aid on his cheek when they joined us. The guys reprised the match blow by blow until I yawned.

"I need to go. It's been a big day." I hugged Magda and Lena, told 'em I'd see them tomorrow at the show. I went to sleep that night thinking of my new acquisition, and glad the drama was all over. I looked forward to the next day and to taking home Judy's quilt.

Chapter 42

Scandal at the Willamina Quilt Show

Day two started quietly enough with Dan and I dawdling away much of the morning. We didn't get to the Show until near eleven. I visited my *Peace*. It pleased me even more than it had the day before. I spent good time shopping, buying sturdy potholders and other homemade things for Christmas presents, plus a skirt for my Christmas tree. We went uptown and took tea with the Chamber of Commerce women serving us, ate a quick lunch again with the church ladies, and by one were back at the show.

We examined the prize quilt made by the Guild women. I tried counting stitches on Lena's quilts but found myself going cross-eyed.

The peace shattered with a shout that resounded through the room, "No! This is wrong!" A woman's voice. It came from the far side, back where the specialty quilts were.

Every head turned.

"Damn you, Len!"

I started toward the commotion, turned to say something to Dan behind me, and saw Len. Apparently he'd been in the process of setting up his easel. Now he was headed towards the exit, carrying the framed Kamleika. A woman was behind him, carrying the easel. They weren't making much headway. Their exit was blocked by people going to see what the noise was about.

Without even thinking I caught his upper arm. "I have something to say to you!"

He tried to tug free.

Dan, who was right behind me, stopped him. "The lady said she had something to say to you. Best stay here a moment, and listen." He grinned at Len. "I think there's more to come."

Len plainly didn't want the crowd he'd drawn. But Magda and Sam flanked him on the other side.

Sam said, "Yeah, Flash. I suspect it's your time to hang, and rattle."

I stepped close so I was right in Len's face.

"You said you were divorced. You scum. And the car isn't even yours. You're still a phony. Not many changes from the past, but you're a bigger liar than ever." I took my hand off his arm. "I'm through with him. Let him pass."

"Oh, no." Before Dan, Sam and Magda could step aside, Katie Heap and a tall, striking blonde woman stepped up behind Dan. The blonde's black eyes were fairly snapping. She grabbed Len by the arm I'd just let go of, dragged him toward the back of the room.

"Idiot! How could you think you could get away with this? Think I'd not see it?" All this while she was yanking on him, and he was stumbling along.

We all followed them to the specialty quilts area, where Len's prize winning quilt was hanging. On the tag attached it was printed, large and dark, "Quilt made by Len Bolder."

The woman ripped off the paper.

"Hey. You can't do that!" Magda said.

The woman held Len's arm in a tight grip. She was strong. Len was pale, as he said, "I can explain."

She gave Len's arm another yank. "You're going to tell these people that this signature—L. Bolder—is me, Linda. Not you!"

Linda Bolder. All became clear. Len's wife. Her fury reinforced her demand. "Now."

"Linda, look, it's no big deal. Another chance for people to see your excellent work. I was gonna tell them."

Linda started taking down the quilt. "Sorry," she said to Magda and the other Guild women gathered around. "I'd be proud to have my quilt in your show, but only with my name on it. Len here sometimes gets confused about what's his, and what's mine."

He wouldn't shut up. "We learned how to make that quilt together. So you made it, big deal. I could have. It was an honest mistake, really. Lin, when I picked up your quilt from the Fair I just brought it here. They were confused about who made it. I was going to tell them."

I felt like slapping him. "Nothing honest about it Len. You lied to me about the quilt. And you lied to me about her. Said you'd divorced."

Linda let go of him with a shove, so that he stumbled towards me. "You can have him."

"Hey!" he wailed, ending in a whine, "I just let you think what you wanted to. I didn't lie."

I shoved him back towards her. "He's a piece of scum I don't need to see again." To him I said, "You used me to get your wife's quilt in the show."

Lena stepped up. "Magda, maybe we should call the

police, get this jerk's ass thrown in jail for fraud. I don't like men who are liars." She advanced on him, but Big Juan touched her gently on her shoulder.

"Sweet one, let's let Magda and the girls take care of this one, shall we?" Like coming out of a sudden trance Lena stepped back and flipped her hand at Len. "Let the creep go. We don't need our Quilt Show slimed by the likes of him." She cuddled back into Big Juan's embrace.

"There is the matter of the Kamleika," Katie said, as the entry door opened and Sheriff Kelly and Deputy Bybee walked in. "We didn't come alone."

"Damn!" Len spat. "See what you've done now."

"Don't blame Katie," said Linda. "Once I learned what you were showing here, I called the police. I've chosen to be blind to your behavior, but this is stealing from people who trusted me, as well as committing what is probably a Federal crime. My sister told me about the Kamleika missing from her brother-in-law's house. I never suspected you had it."

The crowd was absolutely silent. Sheriff Kelly stepped up to Len, relieved him of the Kamleika, and handed it off to Linda. "We'll be needing this. Hold on to it until we're done here." Deputy Bybee relieved the girlfriend of the easel. With one hand Sheriff Kelly folded Len's arms behind him, with the other he snapped handcuffs around his wrists. The sound they made when they closed rang through the silence of the hall.

Len's face turned red. "No! This is all a mistake. I can explain!"

The sheriff said, "We've been in touch with the authorities in Alaska and they're eager to talk to you. You're under arrest for theft under the Native Antiquities act of Alaska."

Len stopped struggling and paled as he listened to Sheriff

Kelly read him his rights.

At the end he said, "I want a lawyer. Linda, call our lawyer."

"Sorry, he's my lawyer, now. You can use your one call to find you another one."

Linda almost had the quilt off the frame when Magda caught her hand. "We'd be happy to have your quilt in the show. It's wonderful. We'll make up a new info tag."

Linda stopped, "Okay. I don't blame you. I know how convincing he can be."

I whispered to Magda, "I'm sorry to have dragged you into this."

She whispered back, "Don't worry about it. Gave the show a little extra zip."

The woman who'd been with Len came over and said, to both Linda and me, "I just met him a couple days ago. He seemed like a real nice guy. I'll call a friend to pick me up."

Katie said, "I can give you a ride. Turns out I'll be driving my car that way."

"That would be great. I'll need to pick up my things at the motel. I'll be ready when you are."

From his shirt pocket Dan pulled out his completed Art Tour form. "Whoops, we don't want to forget this." I took mine from my purse and we put the both of them in the collection box.

We stayed to help clean up the show and then went to Sam's and Magda's house to see how *Sweethearts* looked on their bed. It was a perfect fit. I'd swear Sam had a couple of tears, but he quickly wiped them away, so I can't be sure.

"So when am I going to see you again?" Magda said. "What's your next quilt going to be?"

"Next quilt?" I was thinking of a small star quilt to make for a young friend's baby. But after that I'm done with this quilting thing. Maybe one for my bed at home. Our bed? Perhaps. Something special. That will be enough.

Magda's right. The making of this quilt was soothing, but all this other drama? I need for my life to slow down. I've got thinking to do. While I'm thinking I could be making that little quilt.

"I do have some questions about how you make a baby quilt, Magda. I'll be in touch, soon. By the way, what is your address?"

On our way out of town I had Dan stop at the post office where, from my purse I pulled out the "Wish you were here" postcard and wrote on it: *Sam, you lucky old fool, your new home is 'here'. Magda, welcome to the family. You good hearts belong together. Congratulations. Love, Annie & Dan. P.S. We'll be by soon, Dan needs banana bread.*

I put a stamp on it and with a giggle I dropped it in the mail slot.

Once we were on the highway I said to Dan, "Boy, I think we'll win something, don't you? We had lunch there at the church, and went to every store and shop and you even bought me a pretty. We gotta win something, right?"

"Honey, all I can say is, if we don't it'll be a scandal."

THE END

Author's Note

The following books and articles were invaluable to me while I was crafting this story.

Secrets of Eskimo Skin Sewing by Edna Wilder, 1976, Alaska
  Northwest Publishing Company, p. 94-96

The Quilter's Catalog, A Comprehensive Resource Guide by Meg Cox, 2008 Workman Publishing Company, Inc.

Parka (Kamleika) Inuit, (from Wikipedia). http://en.wikipedia.org/wiki/Kamleika

History of the Kayak, (from Wikipedia). www.coastmountainsexpeditions.com/.../history-sea-kayak-artic-mod...

About the Author

I was raised in the Willamette Valley of Portland, Oregon area. I've been writing since the eighth grade. I currently focus on fiction set in Oregon with romantic, mystery, quilting, and historical themes. My non-writing work history is varied, from retail to kitchens. My primary work has been as a counselor. I've lived in big cities, now treasure the simple life, living next to the beach and a wetland. Have lived on both coasts of America, and in the desert, where I attended college. I've married twice, have two children, four grandchildren, all grown. I enjoy traveling with my husband, John Port. I am an Anglophile, love American history as well. When I'm not writing or reading, I'm working in my garden, sewing, cooking, or opening the door for our two cats. I want to build a small chicken house and raise a few chickens.

* * * *

Uncial Press brings you extraordinary fiction, non-fiction and poetry. Put a world of reading in your pocket.

www.uncialpress.com